The Need for Better Regulation of Outer Space

A collection of short stories

The Need for Better Regulation of Outer Space

A collection of short stories

Pippa Goldschmidt

FREIGHT BOOKS

First published in the UK 2015
Freight Books
49-53 Virginia Street
Glasgow, G1 1TS
www.freightbooks.co.uk

A CIP catalogue reference for this book is available from the
British Library.

ISBN 978-1-910449-12-7
ISBN Ebook 978-1-910449-13-4

Typeset by Freight in Plantin & Aktiv Grotesk
Printed and bound by Bell and Bain, Glasgow

the publisher acknowledges investment from
Creative Scotland toward the publication of this book

Pippa Goldschmidt grew up in London and now lives in Edinburgh. Her novel *'The Falling Sky'* is also published by Freight and was runner-up in the Dundee International Book Prize in 2012. She has a PhD in astronomy and was an astronomer for several years at Imperial College. She was awarded a Scottish Book Trust New Writers Award in 2012 and has worked as a writer-in-residence at several academic institutions including most recently the Hanse-Wissenschaftskolleg in Germany. Her short stories, poetry and non-fiction have been broadcast and published in a wide variety of publications including Gutter, New Writing Scotland, and the New York Times as well as in anthologies such as *'The Best American Science and Nature Writing 2014'* and *'Be the First to Like This: New Scottish Poetry'.*

For my family

Contents

Introduction to relativity

14 week course. Some experience of maths required.

Week 1

You're in the front row of the lecture theatre listening to the lecturer. 'Alice is travelling on the train, flashing her torch at Bob who is standing on the station platform.'

You haven't had this lecturer before, he must be new. You shift in your seat and sure enough, he looks at you. There is a minute pause, the merest stutter in his words that is undetectable to anyone else, as you watch him analyse the geometry of your blouse.

You wonder whether Alice regularly rides around on trains flashing her torch at men. You picture her in a plastic mac and high-heeled boots. You wonder what Bob gets out of this arrangement, perhaps he fancies Alice.

'Alice sees the torchlight expand equally in all directions, hitting the front and back of the train at the same time.' The other students are writing this down in their notebooks. You doodle a heart on the cover of yours, and consider undoing another button on your blouse.

'But Bob sees the light strike the back of the train before the front. Can anyone tell me who is right? Alice or Bob?' Silence. You glance at the other students before putting up your hand, and he nods at you to speak.

'They're both right. From Bob's point of view the back of the train has travelled towards the light and the front has travelled away from it. So he sees the light reach the back of the train before it reaches the front. But Alice is travelling with the train and to her the front and back of the train aren't moving. So for her, the light strikes the front and back at the same time.'

You pause. 'They're both right,' you repeat.

He nods again before continuing, 'The speed of light is a constant, and that leads to different versions of reality. All are equally valid.' You like this. Brusque and efficient. You continue to doodle hearts as he lectures.

Week 2

You feel a bit sorry for Bob. He never goes anywhere, just stands around on station platforms waiting for Alice to communicate with him. She gets all the fun. You've noticed that the other students write down everything the lecturer says, but they can't answer any of his questions. You don't need to write anything down because you've done all this stuff before. You like the way he looks at you now when he asks a question, as if he expects something from you.

His wedding ring glints in the artificial light of the lecture theatre. You stroke the buttons on your blouse.

Week 3

Alice is in a lift, plummeting to Earth. The lecturer says she doesn't feel anything as she falls, not even gravity, but you're pretty sure she might feel terrified. Bob is probably still waiting for her on a platform somewhere, wondering where she is. Poor, faithful Bob. What an idiot.

There are fewer students now. That always happens at this point in the course. They can't take it. The extrapolation from the everyday stuff: the clocks, trains and torches, to the imaginary: inertial forces, curved space-time, and the vacuum. You're used to it. You can cope.

At the end of the lecture, when the other students are shuffling out, the lecturer walks over to you. You cover the front of your notebook so he can't see the hearts.

'You never write anything down.' Again, that brusqueness.

'I don't need to,' and you smile and walk off.

Week 4

You're given coursework: *'Quantify Newton's error in his derivation of Mercury's orbit around the Sun, and show how Einstein was able to correct this error in the context of general relativity.'*

This is standard textbook stuff. You're almost disappointed that the lecturer appears to show such little imagination. You hope he's more imaginative in other aspects of his life. You email the answer to him and you don't have to wait long for his reply. He wants to see you, in his office. It's taken a week longer than usual, but that doesn't matter. There's still plenty of time.

You've been to the office before, when the last lecturer had it. This one's rearranged the furniture, but the rug's in the same place. You remember the rug.

'There is a practical element to the coursework,' he tells you, 'you must choose an experiment and I need to approve it.'

You suggest a quick, straightforward experiment, one that you and he can carry out on the floor of the office. He agrees.

Week 5

Alice is now in a spaceship, travelling around the Universe at almost the speed of light while, as usual, Bob waits for her back at home. You suspect Bob doesn't look so hot now, with all that waiting around for Alice and worrying about her.

'Who can explain why Bob ages faster than Alice?' He's wearing a nice shirt today, crisp and ironed, presumably by his wife. You imagine running your hands up his arms, along the ridge of his shoulders and down his chest, feeling the heat of his body.

There are only three other students in the lecture hall today. The lecturer waits for you to answer, but you stay silent. You don't see why you should do all the work.

Week 6

You suggest to the lecturer that your experiment should be repeated, to make sure you can get the same result as before. He agrees. Afterwards, in the lecture theatre, his shirt looks a little crumpled.

Space-time has been compressed by your experiment. The lecturer is standing in front of the white board, picking his way along an equation, and he's also lying stretched out on the rug, a sheen of sweat still visible on his stomach.

The experiment starts to be repeated regularly, sometimes twice a day. In his office, he shuts the door behind you and tips your head back to kiss your throat.

Week 7

The lecturer introduces Carol to Bob and Alice. Carol is more adventurous than either of them. She falls into black holes, where she gets stretched into string by warped space-time, and becomes cut off from the rest of the Universe. As she sends out a last message before she sinks below the event horizon, Bob and Alice see a static vision of her, forever poised above it.

You can also see her. She's wearing your favourite jeans, the ones the lecturer ripped in his hurry to get them off you. You're wearing them again today, in spite of the tear in the fabric. You're hoping he'll notice them and remember.

Week 8

The lecturer deviates from the course material and talks about dark matter. You can picture it slipping around the Universe, fastening itself to discrete objects. You already know how quick it is to react to certain forces, such as the proximity of a hand, or the unbuttoning of a blouse.

'Dark matter fills the Universe,' he tells you and the other students, 'it doesn't interact with light, only with mass.'

You trace a spiral with your finger on the desk; thinking about the slow, sweet curve of bodies as they orbit around each other, before falling inwards. But his wedding ring is gold, and although it's soft enough to show your teeth marks, it will last until the Earth and Moon finally plunge into the Sun.

Week 9

His wife is pregnant. He shows you the scan of the baby, its head arched in profile as if already searching the starless space around it for answers. Now, you don't know what to say. Now, as he pulls you towards him to get at your throat, you wonder what will happen in the future. You're not used to thinking like this. These courses are completely predictable. That's the best thing about them.

The next piece of coursework is about mass and its dependence on speed. As objects travel faster, they get more massive. You think that maybe Bob won't find Alice so attractive now that she's getting heavier and her ankles are fat. Your calculation shows that he should always prefer Carol, but you get the answer wrong. This is the first time this has happened to you. You question the lecturer about it, but he's able to show a mistake in your logic.

Week 10

This week he's onto entropy, and the growth of disorder and decay as time moves from the past to the future. This contradicts relativity, which doesn't depend on time. You hoped relativity would win out over entropy, but you know what entropy is now.

Now, after each experiment, he picks the fluff from the rug off his clothes, smoothes his hair, and sniffs himself before he sends you out of his office. He has work to do; other courses to write. You find it difficult to concentrate on your own work. You are not sure what else to do apart from the experiment. You thought that would be enough for this course.

Week 11

The next deviation occurs. He talks about calculating the orbits of bodies. A two-body problem is analytical. Once the initial conditions are known, the entire future of the orbit is known. But if there are three bodies, the system becomes uncertain. The effect of any perturbation on this system, however tiny, can't be predicted in advance. It can only be observed.

You check through your notes. You don't know this material, previous courses haven't covered it. He shouldn't be talking about it.

When you are both lying on the rug in his office, you ask him why he is making changes. His shirt and trousers are still open, but his skin reveals nothing.

'Nothing stays the same,' he says finally. He stares straight ahead when he speaks, not looking at you. 'Nothing should stay the same.'

Clocks, trains and torches are always there. Carol, Bob and Alice are always there. You lean over to touch him, but all you can reach are his fingertips.

Week 12

Entropy means that things change, orbits decay. Planets spiral into stars and are annihilated. As they do so, they send out gravitational waves; beacons of distress emitted across the Universe.

He doesn't have much time any more, so the experiment is stripped down to the essentials. He doesn't bother with kissing your throat.

'Is this happening at the same time?' you ask, afterwards.

'The same time as what?'

At the same time for both of us, you think, but there is no point in saying it, not now. You should have said it before, at the beginning, when he did have time.

'I have to go,' he says, and he hands you your bra as if

he doesn't want to see your breasts any more. You feel like weeping. You consider refusing to accept it, abandoning it here as definitive evidence. Now that there is a past to this, and maybe not a future, you want someone else to see your bra hanging from his chair, and know what has happened here. You're not the observer of this experiment any more. Perhaps you never were.

Week 13

Bob has surprised everyone and bought a motorbike. It's his turn to accelerate to the speed of light. Alice isn't allowed to join him. As he roars along the motorway the light he emits settles into a sort of cloud around him, shielding him from everything else in the Universe, even Carol.

When you walk along the corridor to the lecturer's office, the door is shut. He's either not there, or he is there. You don't know which is worse.

Week 14

The lecturer puts his notes into his briefcase, and leaves without looking at you. The course is over and the only other student is asleep at the far end of the lecture theatre. All you can do is follow the lecturer to his office. He has told you that you must keep a certain distance as you walk behind him, and that nobody must see as you follow him inside. You must not disturb anything, apart from yourself. Those are the rules of this experiment.

Week 15

You sign up for a different course next term. You hope the next lecturer will be pleased at your understanding of the subject. You hope your coursework will be satisfactory.

The first star

When we measure the stars on photographic plates, the first star on each plate is the reference to which all the other ones must be compared. I think of the first star as a bit like the head girl of a school. The head girl has the shiniest hair, the most upright comportment, the gentlest smile. She does not speak until spoken to, and when she answers questions, does so in a low and pleasing voice.

When I was at school, I could not be the head girl. I did not measure up to that standard, although I was good at my lessons, particularly mathematics, which is how I come to be here. Working as a computer at the Royal Observatory on Blackford Hill.

Mr Storey, who is assistant to the Astronomer Royal, visited the school although at that time I did not know who he was. I first noticed him waiting outside the headmistress's office because it was a sunny day and he took off his jacket and rolled up his shirtsleeves, as if he were at home after work and waiting for his wife to bring him his dinner. He did not see me looking at him, so perhaps that is why he felt he could do that. People generally do not notice me looking at them, which may be another reason why I was not suited to becoming head girl.

All summer term we had been talking about what might become of us when we left and had to make our own way in the world. Most of us were likely to be schoolteachers although I had a secret dread of that profession, because if I had to continue attending school as an adult then it would feel as if time had simply stood still. Especially as I had no money for new clothes and so would have to wear my old school dress.

But then I saw the rolled up shirtsleeves of Mr Storey, and wondered about him. Perhaps he was a clerk, or a bookkeeper. I was not far wrong in being enticed by the shirtsleeves, except it is myself who is a sort of bookkeeper, because after we measure each star we must enter its details into a large book; its coordinates in the left-hand column and its stellar classification in the right-hand one.

Stars have many classifications, from blue to red and most colours in between. It is a shame we do not see the colours on the photographic plate. But you can tell by the shape, the swell of the spectrum, whether its light is emitted towards the left end (blue) or the right end (red). I should like to see the true colours of the stars with my own eye as they appear through the telescopes here. But we leave work each evening at 5pm, as we are not allowed on the hill at night. Only the astronomers may look through the telescopes, and we cannot work with them. So I can only imagine what they see. It is not hard imagining, like constructing a sort of heaven. We were taught about the pearly gates at school and now I can picture them as dotted all over with different coloured stars.

As I watched Mr Storey tilting his face to the sun to soak up the warmth, the headmistress opened her door and peered out, and he pulled on his jacket in a hurry and disappeared inside. I continued to wait, ignoring the bell ringing for the afternoon's lessons, and then I decided to wander towards the office. As I got there the door opened again, and the headmistress saw me and gestured for me to enter.

This was my first time in all the time at school that I had been invited into that office, and I thought it was very beautiful. The walls were a clean pale blue, as if the summer sky had been allowed to enter and take up residence. There were two china cups set on a wooden table, the headmistress and Mr Storey must have had tea together. The rest of the school was full of chalk dust and inkblots and little girls crying, but in here I felt a million miles away from all of that.

'I saw you waiting and watching,' was the first thing Mr Storey said to me, so I was embarrassed and realised that perhaps I can be seen even when I think I cannot, 'what were you waiting for?'

'You, sir,' which was a bit forward, and I didn't know why I said that. But it was true, I was waiting for him to decide something for me. And it worked because he laughed.

'This is one of our best girls,' said the headmistress. 'Her mathematical abilities are outstanding.'

Mr Storey nodded his head. 'And would you like to earn a shilling each day?'

I said yes.

'Good. That's settled then.'

But I had no idea what it was that they wanted me to do for the shilling, and they didn't tell me.

The day I started working at the Observatory I sat on the bus and arranged my dress very carefully around me so as not to crease it, and I peered out of the window the whole journey so I would not miss my stop at Blackford station. I walked up the hill slowly, I did not know what was waiting for me at the top and still nobody had told me. Of course I could see the Observatory towers, with their green metal tops, anyone can see them from the centre of the city. When I got there, I saw that beside the towers and the long building connecting them, there was also a large villa off to one side. As I stood at the Observatory's entrance waiting for Mr Storey, a maid came out of the villa with a basket of wood. She saw me and stopped, and for a moment I wished I was her so that I would know what to do and where to go. And then that feeling went. I am an adult now, I told myself, and I will have to get used to not knowing things.

And at first when I was shown the photographic plates it all felt very odd, and I was very aware of every little thing that

I was being asked to do, but I should think anything is odd after so many years at school. Being married would also feel quite odd.

By the time the other girls started a few days after me, I knew the routine. I knew to handle the photographic plates only by the edges to avoid touching the emulsion, I knew to set them down on the table so that north is pointing up and east is to the left. I even knew why that was so: compass directions on the sky are a mirror image of those on Earth and everything is facing the wrong way. Mr Storey told me this on the first day.

The photographic plates are like nothing I have ever seen before. They are big square pieces of glass, but so thin that they can bend under their own weight. Because they are negatives, the sky is white and the stars are black. There are usually about a handful of stars on each plate, but they do not look like proper solid objects because they have been smeared out into black lines by a prism in the telescope. Mr Storey told me that each black line has its own characteristic, it may be thicker or thinner than its neighbours, it may swell at one end or it may even show white gaps. I think of these as gaps in the black fences of the stars.

Mr Storey oversees us, which is some feat because he works many nights and then comes to this office in the morning as we remove our coats and make our cups of tea (we have a kettle for the fire). He sets out the plates for us and decides what we look at, what is important and what is not. He teaches us how to position the eyepiece over the plate and focus it so that the stars become clear and sharp. At the beginning Mr Storey stood behind me as I tried to work the eyepiece. When I couldn't do it he would reach around me and taking my right hand he would ease it round the dial. 'Gently,' he would say, 'just gently.'

'That's why we hired you girls,' he said, 'because you have the right touch.'

I have never been that near to a man before and at first it

didn't seem right to have him close enough that I could feel his breath on my hair and cheek. Hear him whisper those words at me, 'Gently, just gently.'

'A boy couldn't do it. You need a lady's fingers on those controls,' he would say.

He always has his shirtsleeves rolled up so I can see the smooth skin on his arms. I never knew men looked like that.

Now I know how to do it, so he doesn't need to stand behind me anymore. Flora still has problems though, and he still helps her. My mother didn't like it when I told her about Mr Storey helping us in that way, so I stopped telling her.

Sometimes when my neck hurts from looking down at the plates I allow myself to glance up and away, out of the window. You can forget about the greenness of grass if you stare at black lines all day. Outside children play and the Astronomer Royal's wife stands nearby gazing up at the sky, as if trying to estimate whether it will be clear tonight and whether her husband will be eating his supper with her and the children, or working on the telescope.

I don't think she can see her husband very often, for he teaches the university students during the day, and works at the telescope at night. I wonder if she hopes for cloudy nights and then feels guilty.

She is good to us, she gives us bread and jam sometimes and asks our opinion of it, it seems she is writing a cookbook about jam and is trying different recipes. I enjoy them all so cannot really advise her. We do not have much jam at home, so I would like to buy a pot from her but I am nervous about suggesting it. She might not like the idea.

She has the groceries delivered to the Observatory twice a week, and I feel sorry for the horse making its way up that steep hill, laden with goods. The hill starts off gradual and then becomes harder and harder, like a mathematical test.

Sometimes I look at the maid wrestling the sheets onto the

line and am grateful I am not her. The maid stays up here at the Astronomer Royal's house but she must be exhausted by night-time and in her bed before the stars are out.

There are three of us computers; myself, Flora and Jeanie. Flora is my age and Jeanie is a bit older. She has been a teacher but thinks this is better work, quieter and more peaceful. She says the children gave her dreadful headaches. Flora finds it difficult to walk up the hill, and arrives red-faced and perspiring each morning. When it is warm outside, she has a strong smell about her by the end of the day. But they are nice girls and we do well together in our little room, with Mr Storey to guide us.

I asked them what would happen when we finished looking at all the stars and they laughed at me.

'The stars do not end,' said Jeanie, 'they go on forever.'

'Nonsense,' said Flora, 'they must end, but there are still so many of them that we will have enough work for the rest of our lives.'

Even though they could not agree on the number of stars, I was very relieved at the thought of being able to stay here, for I do not know what else I could do apart from teaching. Or even worse, being a governess. My friend from school, Agnes, is a lady's companion now and she said it is quite agreeable but the lady does go on at her so about her manners and style. She is not required to do much other than accompany the lady to other ladies' houses and sit silently while they gossip about yet more ladies. It sounded deadly dull to me, but when I tried to tell her about my work, she said looking at black lines all day was very peculiar and would make her feel faint.

I do not think it is peculiar. The stars must be so far away that it seems remarkable to me we can look at them and turn them into black lines, and then into numbers. It is like magic. Except this is science, which is supposed to be the opposite of magic.

I asked Mr Storey if we could look at the planets in the same way on our photographic plates but he said no. I was asking him because I wanted to have a proper scientific conversation with him, the way that I have overheard him talk with the Astronomer Royal, although I am not even sure what a planet really is. But sometimes when I walk home down the hill in winter and the stars are already out (although it is very cold and I wrap up my face against the east wind) I can see Jupiter – a big yellow ball.

Mr Storey takes away our books once a week. I would like to know what he does with them. It seems odd entering all these numbers for someone else to read and understand. I wonder if the Astronomer Royal himself studies our books. He does not talk to us.

On the bus this morning I saw a man reading a newspaper and on the front was a photograph of a large fire reaching up to the sky. I could not see the headline of the newspaper so I asked the man what had happened. He was very young and nervous-looking, otherwise I would not have dared speak.

'The racecourse at Ayr was set on fire.' He spoke so quietly it was little more than whispering, so I smiled to encourage him. 'It's a disgrace, that's what it is,' he added, still in a whisper.

'What is?'

'These suffragettes. All this damage. They all ought to be locked up, every single one of them. They cannot be real women.' He didn't once look at me as he spoke, but kept his eyes downwards, looking at the photograph of the fire. His hand was clamped around the newspaper so firmly that I saw the knuckles were white. Perhaps he was worried that the photograph might escape and set fire to something else. And it struck me that I look at fire every day, for Mr Storey told us that the stars are great globes of fiery gas.

This morning as I walk up the hill I see a puff of smoke in the distance, in the north of the city. And then another, nearer. And then a bang, as if someone has let off a firework, but there are no sparks, just smoke and everything else is still and silent. Up here you can see all the greyness of Edinburgh spread around in front of you. It is a heavy city, there is no lightness in the buildings.

So I wonder if this smoke is from a fiery dragon walking the streets and eating small children and I smile to myself, thinking that Jeanie will be amused by this. Why are women supposed always to like children, or to want them? And have to spend all their days, unless they are rich enough to avoid it by employing maids, taking care of children, whether it be at home or in a school?

I am the eldest in our family so I have had more than my share of mopping mouths smeared with food and wiping sticky fingers and dealing with soiled nappies. That is why I am not so concerned about courting and young men. They cannot tell me about the stars or help me learn new ways of seeing things.

Flora and Jeanie think otherwise. 'You do not really want to be a spinster,' they say.

'Why not?' I pour the hot water into the teapot as we wait for Mr Storey to appear and tell us which plates to work on. 'Many of us will be spinsters anyway, there are not enough men. And you have forgotten about the children. If we are married there will have to be children.'

The Astronomer Royal's children are running about the hill right now, as I wait for the tea to brew. We all like it strong. I can hear them screaming, they scream a lot.

Flora and Jeanie don't answer that. I stir spoonfuls of condensed milk into each cup of tea. This is a good time of day, for I always hope I will find a different sort of star, one with its gaps in a different place. Nearly all the stars have the gaps in the same place, they are just big or little gaps. I asked Mr Storey why the gaps were in the same place and he could not answer. He said that it was a good question but he did not know. Perhaps stars are like faces and they need their equivalent of eyes, nose and mouth in the right order.

Normally he is so steady, but when he arrives today he looks a bit flustered. 'Did you hear the noises, girls?'

We nod.

'Bombs, that's what it was.'

'Bombs?' I can't imagine what he was talking about. 'What do you mean?'

The word itself feels heavy on my tongue, like something slipping beneath the surface of dark water. Not at all to do with fire and smoke.

But he doesn't answer me properly, he just says, 'I fought in the war and I know the sound of explosives. I never thought I would hear that sound at home.'

He busies himself with his tea and I wonder which war he means. Probably the second Boer war, which was when I was very young. Nobody talks about it much now, even though there was all that excitement over Mafeking and Baden-Powell. People do forget things very quickly, or maybe they are just waiting for the next war. For there will be one soon, as everybody knows. Perhaps this is it.

'Are the bombs the start of a new war?' I ask him, 'are we at war?'

'Silly girl, you don't know what you're talking about,' he puts down his teacup rather too quickly and the handle breaks off on his fingers.

I stare at that loop of china made all blurry by the tears in my eyes. He has never called me silly before. But men are funny about their wars, they act as if they own them, and perhaps they do, for I don't think women ever start them.

'Which plates are we to measure today?' I ask him, trying to sound efficient. I have never had to ask him this before, and he looks around him as if trying to work out why he is there.

He lays the broken handle on our work table, 'I do not think there are any plates today,' he says slowly, and I feel very afraid because I think that I have been right all along and we have been too quick in our measuring, me and Flora and Jeanie, and come to the end of all the stars and will lose our jobs. I begin to regret working so quickly, but I wanted to please him. And the Astronomer Royal.

'Last night's plates are not yet developed and there are no others. Look – why don't you have a day's holiday? We will pay you as usual and you can do what you like, go look at the shops.'

Flora and Jeanie seem delighted at this, but I just think, well I have walked up the hill and am not so keen to walk down it and take a bus into town to look at things in shops that I cannot afford. And I don't want to go home and help with the children again.

They are already putting on their coats and looking ready to leave but I say, 'Is there nothing else that I can do that might be helpful to you?'

'I don't think so,' and he looks like he might almost laugh at my enthusiasm so I feel a bit blurry around the eyes again. I don't want him to see so I fetch my coat.

Flora and Jeanie go off to Jenners to see the new spring hats. I do not care about hats so I wander into the Old Town. I am keen to learn more about this morning's explosions. And soon I find a building which has holes where its windows once were, and there is a neat pile of glittery glass on the pavement. I peer through the window holes, inside it is very dark and scorched-looking, with black soot marks spreading up the walls, and pictures hanging all crooked. A policeman is standing by the pile of glass so I walk over to him.

'What happened?'

He looks at me suspiciously, 'and why would you want to know, Miss?'

'I heard the noise this morning. Was it bombs?'

This last word seems to be the right one for he flushes deep red. 'Away with you,' he says and flaps his hand at me, 'off you go, young lady.'

The building itself seems to be a ruin now. It's impossible to imagine that it was ever anything else. Perhaps bombs are machines for speeding up what time always does anyway. For making us travel from the past into the future.

The next morning when I get to the bottom of the hill and prepare myself for the daily battle with its curves, I am surprised to see another policeman.

'Where are you going, Miss?' he asks me.

'Up there,' I gesture at the towers, 'I work at the Observatory.'

He raises his eyebrows, 'A maid? Go on, then, they'll be expecting you.'

'No, I'm not a maid,' I mutter but he doesn't hear and I am so curious about why there should be a policeman standing guard by the arch that I get up the hill in record time.

As I round the bend near the top, all is commotion. The children race around, as normal, but the Astronomer Royal and Mr Storey are also pacing back and forth, pointing at the West Tower and at the ground. I walk over to the two men, picking my way across some broken bricks and masonry which are scattered all over the grass. A large crack has appeared in the brickwork at the base of the tower so that anyone can look in, at pieces of twisted metal and smashed glass. It is like peering into an animal's insides, and seeing everything all exposed. Somehow it is worse than the exploded building in the Old Town. Nearby is another policeman, writing something in a notebook.

Mr Storey is the first to notice me, 'Hullo! Look what has happened to our tower!'

'What caused it?' I ask, but I already know. There is the smell here too, the smell from yesterday. Something violent has happened here.

The Astronomer Royal turns around and sees me, 'Who are you?' he asks and he doesn't look very friendly. I always imagined having a conversation with him about the stars and our work, but before I can reply, he says, 'I need to inspect the damage inside. I fear the clock may have taken the brunt of it.'

I watch him walk away, and he seems to stumble over something lying on the ground, and then he kicks it. I see a flash of light as he sends a bit of broken glass flying through the air before it hits the ground again and breaks up into even smaller fragments.

Behind Mr Storey I can see Flora and Jeanie struggling up the hill. They are still some way off so I will have a few moments alone with him before they arrive. 'What happened?' I ask.

'Our work is destroyed,' he glares at me, 'all destroyed by the actions of stupid women.'

'Do you know why they did it?' I am keen to understand the reasons behind this action. I know the suffragettes are bombing railway carriages, slashing paintings in galleries, and destroying postboxes. I know they are doing this because they want the vote. But why did they come up here, to the Observatory? But my question just makes him even crosser.

'Why?' Even now, when he seems to be angry with me I notice how very green his eyes are. I wish I could stop noticing all these little things about him because they are no use to me. 'Why?' he repeats, 'because they are not true women. They are false, hysterical. They are not ruled by decency or by sense.'

Jeanie and Flora appear, and they gaze at all the debris, round-eyed.

'It was a bomb,' I tell them before Mr Storey can say anything, 'the suffragettes have done it.'

The Astronomer Royal appears again, holding a large broom. 'Make yourself useful,' he says, and he hands me the broom.

He is right, I suppose, we may as well help. So I start to

sweep, and Flora and Jeanie stack the broken bricks into neat piles. As I sweep, the maid appears. She stands on the edge of the drying green with the basket of laundry at her feet and watches. I feel like calling out to her but I don't know what I would say. I have never spoken to her before now. But it seems she watches us very carefully the whole time we are sweeping, and the laundry is forgotten.

Later, we make tea in our little room. We sit and drink it and talk about what we should do now. I am still hopeful that everything will be put back to how it was, all the damage will be mended, and we will be allowed to continue with our plates but the others are not so sure.

'There may not be any more plates. The telescope itself may be destroyed,' Flora gets up and peers out of the window but you cannot really see very much of the rest of the Observatory from our room, so she returns to her tea.

Jeanie is doing calculations on a scrap of paper. 'I can last three weeks on my savings,' she announces, and I realise that I have made no provision for the future. I have given my mother nearly all my earnings, and spent the remainder on bus fares and biscuits.

Mr Storey comes in to the room just as we are admiring Jeanie's neat sums. 'I need to see your hands,' he says. We look at him. As usual, his shirtsleeves are rolled up, but even though I try not to look at his arms I can't help noticing dirt smeared on their undersides. He is usually so clean.

'Our hands?' I automatically look down at my hands waiting in my lap for their next instructions, like pale, obliging creatures. 'Why?'

'Never mind why!' he is shouting, and we are not used to this from Mr Storey, he is not being gentle with us now, 'just show me your hands!'

This is not the way it was, with his hand carefully cupped round mine and both of them moving together around the dial. Now he grabs my fingers and turns my hands palm up as if looking for hidden sweets. Perhaps he thinks we have stolen something. He is rough with my hands, he squeezes my fingers before dropping them. Then he inspects Jeanie's. Then Flora's.

'Ah!' he points to something on Flora's right hand, 'what is this?'

I look at it, and as Flora stays silent, perhaps because she is too frightened to speak I answer him myself, 'It is a graze, Mr Storey. A small cut.'

'Ah!' he says again, 'and caused by what?'

'Caused by the washing tub, sir,' Flora has found her voice, 'I cut myself on my mother's washing tub.'

I am angry now, even as I watch Mr Storey drop Flora's injured hand and hide his eyes behind his own fingers, as if he is ashamed of what he has just done. 'Do you think, Mr Storey,' I say, perhaps a bit too loudly for that small room, 'do you think that when we are not at work here we simply fold ourselves up in a cupboard and wait for the next day to look at some more of your plates?'

He doesn't reply and Jeanie and Flora are staring at me. But I may as well continue, 'When we get home we must all help our mothers, and look after our younger siblings. We cook, we clean, we wash. Why –' because it really is very odd and now the flush of anger has obviously left him, I can dare to ask him, 'why are you inspecting our hands?'

'Because we have found blood.' He looks at me and I have the odd feeling that this is the first time that he has actually seen me in all the time I have been working here, 'The woman who did this must have cut herself. There are drops of blood scattered on the ground behind the tower and all along the path down the back of the hill.'

When I ride the bus home that evening the story is in the newspapers, accompanied by a photograph of the Observatory.

Whoever did it left behind a handbag with some safety pins and currant biscuits wrapped in paper. I try to imagine fire flickering around the tower and flames reaching up to the sky, but all I can think of is a woman running from the damage, shedding blood all along the way, and wondering what will happen next.

And now, nearly two years later, I am still here. Flora and Jeanie have both left to work in the munitions factories and I am in charge of the new girls because Mr Storey has left too. I lay out the plates each morning and then sometimes I leave them busy at their work and walk over to the West Tower. The only reminders of that morning in the spring of 1913 are a new clock for the telescope and a narrow seam of pale brickwork in the tower wall. It's easier to feel than to see, so I run my hands along it, thinking of Mr Storey who has gone to fight in France.

Today, after my visit to the mended tower, I take the book of stellar classifications to the Astronomer Royal. I have an idea for checking the accuracy of our work that I need to discuss with him.

How accurate do you need to be (to get on in life)?

At first Catherine is pleased. Pleased they've chosen her to do the interview on the news about their discovery. It's a good piece of work and she's contributed to it. The closest documented near-miss yet by an asteroid, due to pass between Earth and the belt of satellites only thirty-six thousand kilometres above our heads. The astronomical equivalent of a car roaring past you on the motorway at a hundred miles per hour and missing you by a whisker.

They like this metaphor. The team developed it over coffee in the canteen, just after they submitted the paper and realised it was going to be a big story. They deserve this attention in the media. They've all worked hard. Although to be honest some of them have worked harder than others. And no-one else was there when Catherine sat in the telescope control room at four in the morning calculating the orbit of the faint object she'd just detected, but that's to be expected. She's the most junior member of this team and that's how it works.

Which is why she's pleased when they decide it'll be her doing the TV interview.

'Why not?' they say, and they look at her. They're used to looking at objects. It's what they all do, as part of their work. Inspect the rocky surfaces of barren planets, the fizzing spectra of stars dying above the Earth, the imperfect shapes of galaxies rushing away as if they couldn't bear to be in the same universe.

Above everyone's heads the asteroid gets closer. Every ten minutes, about the length of the planned interview, it travels another few hundred kilometres closer to Earth. Its closest encounter is due to happen in six months.

It will miss the Earth. That is the crucial thing that Catherine has calculated. Because if it doesn't, if it grazes the upper atmosphere, like a stone skimming the surface of a pond, then it will lose speed and fall inwards.

Tunguska, Siberia, 1908. The last documented major impact. In the photo, the forest of pine trees look like matches scattered on a pub table. This one would be larger, much larger.

But she's shown it's all ok, it's not going to happen. Not this time round anyway. Perhaps on its next swing past the Earth in fourteen years something might have perturbed it, made it curve in towards us. It wouldn't take much, just something relatively small, to change the asteroid's orbit and make it dangerous. But they're not so bothered about that. They're not taking the long view. They've got their careers to think about, and this exciting near miss will do them just fine.

Anyway, it's all been double-checked.

'Are you sure?' they asked, the day she talked them through her observations and all the maths, 'are you sure it's going to miss?'

'Yes. Yes, I'm sure.' Of course, she's checked it, several times. A few times at the telescope when she couldn't believe what she'd found. Once on the plane home, still drunk with tiredness after the long observing run. And then finally at her desk early one morning, before she'd gone to the rest of the team to announce it and show them the image that can now be seen on all the websites.

'Perhaps we'd better check as well. Can't be too careful!'

So they redo her estimate of the orbit and she's proved right. There's only a 0.01% chance of her, of them all, being wrong and the asteroid plunging into the Earth.

When the paper's published Catherine is surprised to see that she's not first, or second or even third author. She's much lower down in the lists of names.

'It's alphabetical,' they say. 'On account of it being such a large team.'

'But only three of us actually did any work.'

'Yes, but A was awarded the grant which supports the whole team, B wrote the original telescope proposal (even though he didn't go observing with you on that run when you discovered it), C is an editor on the journal and that's helped us get the paper published so quickly, D has got a slot at a major conference to talk about it next Summer, and we'd like E to come and work with us. E's done some important work in this area.'

She's lucky to be K, she supposes. At least she's not Z. She's never even heard of Z. Perhaps Z is someone's cat, added to the list of authors to make a nice round alphabetical number.

Sometimes when they stand outside the team office and discuss where to go for a drink that night, and Catherine has to escape into the ladies to avoid them, she sweeps up her hair so it can't be seen and imagines shaving it off completely. Binding her breasts. If they were cartoon scientists and wore white coats she could make a tent out of hers and hide in it.

The skirt is problematic. Too tight, too short, and it creeps up between her legs as she walks to work, thinking about how she'll describe the moment of discovering the asteroid. The grey and naked piece of rock, born out of the blank night in front of her eyes. She's glad it's not going to end up exploding into the Earth. Some people might call it ugly, but it's hers. It came out of the night, to her.

In the TV studio for the interview, she tries tugging the skirt down but her legs are still feeling rather exposed when she sits opposite the journalist.

'Now,' he says, 'tell us all about your discovery. The

asteroid that isn't going to hit us,' and he laughs so that she realises she's just the light entertainment at the end of the news. After the daily dose of horror, of bombs and debt and proper domestic crises right on their doorstep, the viewers probably deserve something nicer, something restful involving a pretty picture of the night sky. She's not there to be listened to. Or perhaps they've just turned off the telly and she's an empty screen by now.

'Well, it's actually got a lot more interesting since we issued that press release,' and she shifts in her chair, 'we've received new information, more data.'

'New –'

Catherine cuts him off, 'It seems we were a bit too optimistic in our earlier calculations.' It occurs to her that she's still using the collective noun signifying collective responsibility, and now might be a good time to stop. 'I've redone all the work,' she says, 'all of the sums, and I can say with confidence that there's a more than 10% chance that the asteroid will hit Earth.'

He visibly gulps and looks down at his notes, 'Is that a lot?'

'Well, it's significant,' she smiles kindly, he can't help knowing nothing about statistics.

'And what would happen if it did hit us?'

'All I can say is, don't book your holiday for next year yet!' she laughs as if she's just made a particularly witty joke at a cocktail party. The skirt goes with the laugh. So there was a reason to wear it, after all. Then she stops laughing, because she hasn't finished. This is the most important bit, 'An asteroid that size slamming into Earth will be like a nuclear bomb going off. It could destroy an entire city the size of –' she can't think for a moment, 'well, this city.'

He's gone a bit grey. 'Can you be a bit more definite? When will we know for sure whether it's going to –'

'Oh,' and she looks at her watch as if she's working out the times of buses, 'as it gets nearer we'll be able to take more precise measurements of its orbit. Say, in about three months, we should know one way or another.'

'One way or another...' he repeats.

Afterwards, as she treats herself to a taxi home, she imagines that blast. She can picture the fireball in the sky and the impartial raining down of debris on everyone below. Every last detail is so clear.

The Snow White paradox

Cambridge 1948

I propose to consider the question 'Can
machines think?' Imagine the following
situation, you may recognise it as a party
game. I will refer to it as the imitation
game. A man whom I will label A, and a
woman, B, each go into separate rooms and
they can only communicate to the outside
world by written notes. They are each asked
a series of questions by a third person,
C, who has the job of reading the written
notes and deciding who is the genuine
woman and who is pretending.

Alan Turing pauses to look out of the window at the students
cycling up and down the street, before turning back to his
typewriter:

I propose that the woman, B, is replaced by
a machine. So, C has to judge who is better
at imitating a woman, a man or a machine.
If C decides that the machine is a better
imitator than the man, then the machine
can be said to exhibit some sort of human
~~behaviour~~ intelligence.

Later. Light slants in through the pub window, angled by the
beer glasses so that it spreads out all over the wooden table and
spills over the edge onto the floor. Gorgeous, buttery light, like

a blessing. So rich, Alan feels he can catch it in his hands and eat it.

Alan and Neville, sitting with their drinks. It is safe in here, they can be themselves. Although Alan isn't always sure he knows what that means, and Neville's idea of being himself is to wear a feather boa. Sometimes, when he tutors the undergrads in mathematics (his subject) he wears lipstick. This is tolerated in Cambridge, if not exactly encouraged. It helps that Neville is very good at mathematics, although not as good as Alan. Nobody is as good as Alan.

After the pub, they're back in Alan's rooms and Neville takes centre stage. He swathes himself in Alan's dressing gown, lights a cigarette off the feeble gas fire, and strikes an attitude. 'Who am I?' he asks, fluttering his eyelashes.

Alan stays silent.

'Well?' Neville is insistent.

Alan thinks that there's something in the way he squares his shoulders that would make any other man look – well, manly, but on Neville just makes him look even more effeminate.

'Joan Crawford, in *Mildred Pierce*,' Alan stands by the window, flicking through some papers.

'Well done, Miss Observant,' Neville replies, but he sounds a bit piqued at Alan's refusal to enter into the ritual, to enjoy the artifice.

'More gin?' Alan puts his papers aside and uncorks the bottle.

Neville nods, takes a sip and grimaces, 'This is awful stuff, lukewarm and oily. Can't you get anything better?'

'I'm sure you've swallowed worse than that,' says Alan, and then regrets it. That knowing way of talking, with constant referrals – but never by name, never straightforwardly – to the unseen act is not his style. Everybody speaking in a secret code. Normally he leaves that sort of chat to Neville and his friends.

Neville raises his eyebrows at Alan's *double entendre* and takes another sip.

'Do you always do that?' says Alan.

'Do what?'

Take such small sips. Like a woman.'

'Do they? I have no idea how women drink gin. I've never drunk gin with a woman. Unless you count my mother, which personally I don't.'

'Well, they do. And why don't they ever drink beer? Why always gin?'

'That's easy. Gin stops babies,' Neville grins, 'that's why they drink it.'

'Oh,' and Alan makes some notes on a pad of paper.

Neville sighs, 'Can't you stop working, for once in your entire life?' He lets the dressing gown fall coquettishly around his shoulders, and purses his lips in a parody of a kiss.

Neville is really very intelligent, but he hides it well. Lord knows Cambridge is tolerant of his sort of behaviour, in a city full of men and hardly any women ('Unless they're at Girton and hairier than the men' as Neville says) there is, and probably always has been, a wide variety of male behaviour. Even so, Neville is one of the outliers at the extreme end of the spectrum.

Alan lays his notes to one side. 'I've got a new turntable,' he says, 'shall we give it a go?' The turntable is a thing of beauty, a low sleek affair with a glass lid. 'It's called Snow White,' he continues, 'because it looks like a glass coffin.'

As they start to dance Neville whispers into Alan's ear, 'Am I your handsome prince?' For once, Alan won't answer the question and they continue to dip and turn around the room in silence.

'Play the game,' Alan says. Another Friday night in his rooms, and Neville getting tight on his gin again.

'What game?'

'The game where I ask you questions and you have to pretend to be someone else. Imitate them.'

Neville pulls a face, and Alan chuckles, 'Humour me,' he says, 'it's research. Be a woman.'

'A woman? Which one? Princess Elizabeth riding a horse, the barmaid in the Eagle pulling pints, or some prozzie painting on her eye make-up?'

'Any of them. All of them. So, what do you find attractive in a man?'

Neville snickers, 'That's no good, is it? I don't have to pretend to be a woman to answer that.'

'Oh.' Alan looks down at his hands, 'Alright, how do you make a cake?'

'Fruit cake or sponge?'

'Oh, very good. Yes, that's exactly it,' and he writes this down before continuing, 'now, what's the best way of hemming a skirt?'

An hour later and the gin is all gone. Neville's done his best to describe how he would curl his hair, peel an apple, and paint his finger nails. He mimes walking in high heels around the small living room, and asks Alan for a light in a squeaky voice. Alan cups his hand around Neville's as Neville sucks in smoke from the lit cigarette and arches his neck. Such a pale, tender neck, thinks Alan. Not reddened by the sun, like his own. Such smooth skin. Neville has no need of face powder, even though he carries a little compact and can be seen quite often dabbing his nose from it as he sits in the Eagle.

'Be true to me, Oscar,' Neville says now, fluttering his eyelashes.

'Always, Bosie,' Alan smiles. But he has seen Neville walking along the street, arm in arm with another undergraduate. No matter, he is old enough to be realistic about Neville. These things always end. The question is not if, but when.

'But I can think of some better questions than yours, Alan. Such as; how far would you go? Hand up your blouse, in your brassiere, or down your knickers?'

Much later, and Alan and Neville are lying on the bed, both

drunk. Neville's close enough for Alan to smell his breath, synthetically sweet from the lime juice he swigged with the gin.

'Put Snow White on,' Neville whispers, so Alan pads over to the turntable and gently drops the needle down onto the record.

'Have I told you her story? The story of how I fell in love with her?' he says as he settles back on the bed.

'No,' Neville runs his hand through Alan's hair. He's being affectionate tonight so Alan starts his story.

'I saw the film in the last days of the war, when I had a weekend of leave and nobody to spend it with. So I went to London and I decided to go to the cinema.

'Everyone went to the cinema a lot, then. It was the easiest way of escaping the city. Outside the cinema there were just piles of bricks and rubble, and people shuffling around trying to find places to live, enough to eat. Just trying to get by. The old ways of living had all been destroyed, but we hadn't yet worked out the new rules. But inside it was blissfully dark, just like being outside on a cloudy night when the bombers wouldn't bother to strike.'

Neville is restless, 'What's the story, Alan?'

But Alan is in the past now, his eyes shut, remembering the dusty velvet seats of the cinema creaking beneath him. Walking into the cinema, he had passed a child's shoe abandoned on the pavement, a worn, scratched thing. A single shoe in a city at war is never a good sight. He tries not to think what might have happened to the owner of the shoe.

'I watched the girl with hair as black as coal, eyes as blue as a summer's night and lips as red as cherries. I knew what was going to happen, but I was still entranced. It's like clockwork, she has to die because she's so beautiful and young, and the queen is old and jealous. That's the law in fairytale-land. And it has to be death by poison, or wolves or axes. She's –' he pauses here, trying to find the right word, and Neville touches his hand '– perfection when she's in that glass box, because nothing more can harm her. She's as safe as she can be. So really, she should have been grateful to the queen.'

'But she doesn't die,' says Neville.

Alan smiles, 'No, she doesn't die. Although she's not alive either, not for a long time. She has to wait until the prince comes, before she can wake up again. In fact it's an undecidable problem, because you can't tell in advance how long she'll have to stay in that state. There's no way of knowing when the prince will arrive and wake her up.'

'She's neither dead nor alive,' says Neville.

'Both dead and alive,' Alan corrects him, 'at the same time.'

They lie on the bed, at peace, their arms around each other.

'When I came out of the cinema,' Alan needs to finish his story even though he knows Neville isn't interested any more, 'the child's shoe was still lying there so I picked it up. It was red, like the apple in the film.'

He doesn't tell Neville that the true end of the story came earlier, as he cried in the cinema watching Snow White in her glass box. He cried because he was remembering the death of Christopher Morcom at school. Touching his coffin at the funeral was the nearest he ever got to touching Christopher himself. Tears dripped off his face as he remained motionless in the cinema, after the film had finished and the other people had to squeeze past him. And he was left wondering all over again at the absolute and awful illogicality of death and the sudden vanishing of a person's mind, leaving just their physical body. The child's shoe was just an afterthought. Maybe a symbol of Christopher's death, maybe a symbol of a red apple.

'Do you still have it?' Neville mutters, he's half asleep now.

'Somewhere.' But he can't think what he did with it when he returned to Bletchley.

Manchester, 1952
Alan picks his way along the icy pavement trying to avoid the worst of the frozen puddles. The King died the previous

week and all the buildings in this part of the city have black mourning fabric swathed around the windows. He supposes it's blackout left over from the war.

By the time he reaches the police station his feet are too cold to feel anything and his hands can barely grip the door handle.

'I've come to report a break-in,' he announces to the sergeant on duty, 'at my home.'

The policeman looks at him impassively, 'A break-in. And has anything been stolen?'

'Yes. Some money. And a few personal effects.'

The sergeant is wearing a black arm band. They're all in mourning for someone they've never met. He feels the old prickle of pain behind his eyes, he wears an invisible arm band every day of his life for Christopher.

'Personal effects, sir?' The sergeant's modus operandi seems to be to repeat part of what he has just been told. Perhaps it's a test of some kind.

'Yes. I don't know what, exactly. It's difficult to tell because it's all rather a mess. Stuff has been chucked around the house.'

The sergeant makes a tiny note on his blotter, surely not large enough to contain the information he's just been given, 'And when did you discover this – break-in?'

'Just now. This evening when I arrived home from work.' He's feeling oddly breathless after hurrying here from his house even though he's used to running long distances, so a short walk shouldn't present any problems. But the sergeant's deliberate and slow manner of speaking is making him feel as if he's speeding up, like a record that is being played too quickly.

'The thing is –' he takes a deep breath, 'the thing is, I know who did it.'

The sergeant stands up straighter and looks at him properly for the first time, 'Can I have your full name, sir? And your address?'

An hour later and he's talking to two policemen in a little

room. He's grateful for the privacy but he can't understand why it needs both of them. He has all the information they need, all they have to do is go to the address and arrest the man for breaking and entering.

He even feels a kind of pity for Don, for being so short-sighted. Surely Don would know that he could guess who's done this. Only a couple of weeks after they last saw each other and Don spent the night in Alan's house, propped up in his bed watching him get undressed. Watched him take off his watch and cuff-links and put them away carefully in the little ebony box on the bedside table, where there was also a bundle of cash. Before he turned to Don and took him in his arms.

The next morning Don was silent, even as Alan cooked him bacon and poured him tea. And he hasn't seen him since.

Well, he supposes he will see him now, in court. He'll have to give evidence of course, be a witness. In spite of everything he hopes Don won't get a prison sentence. But he would like his cuff-links back.

'And how do you know this character, sir?' The second policeman is smaller, and sharper looking than the first one. They have already asked him this, he can't see why they're asking him again. He tries not to sigh as he explains how he met Don a few months ago in a pub, ('Which pub, sir?' and they write this down too) and invited him back home.

'Why did you invite him back to your house, sir? For what purpose?'

'I wanted to get to know him better. We chatted in the pub and seemed to have a lot in common, so I suppose I wanted to continue our conversation.'

'Forgive me, sir, but you told us that you are an academic?'
Alan nods.

'So may I ask what you had in common with this man? You say he is a labourer?'

He silently curses the British class system, 'Just because one man has been to university and another man has not, doesn't mean they have nothing to say to each other.'

'How long did he stay in your house, sir? That first evening?'

He blinks, remembering Don's unexpectedly pale skin, his unexpectedly tender mouth. 'All night.'

'*All* night?' the policemen look at each other, 'all night, sir?'

'Yes. And then he came back the next night.' And the night after as well. It was only after that that things started to go wrong, that Don seemed to resent something about Alan, about his work maybe, or his house. Then he became sullen and sour, and his mouth became hard.

'And would he have had an opportunity to see your bedroom, sir? To see where you kept your valuables? The cuff-links and so on, that you claim he has taken?'

'Why yes, of course he saw my bedroom. That's where he spent the night.'

The policemen are silent for a moment, 'Thank you, sir. That will be all we need for now.'

'But when are you coming round to my house? To see the evidence? The mess he's made?'

They look at each other, 'That may not be necessary, sir. We think we have everything we need to make an arrest.'

Manchester, 1954

Home from a silent evening in the pub at the end of the road, where Alan was afraid to talk to anyone, in case they start asking him about himself. The consequence of not talking all night is that he's now drunk too much.

    I am a liar.

Alan faces his reflection in the mirror and touches the image in the glass to steady himself. He has been alone for so long now that he is not quite sure if his thoughts are silent or spoken.

    I am a liar.

To take his mind off the image he forces himself to work

through the logic of this statement. Why is it problematic? Because if it's true, then the person making the statement is a liar, which means it's false. If it's false and the person making it is not a liar, then it's true. So it's neither true nor false. Neither fish nor fowl. But perhaps it's too late for lessons on logic, and he's too drunk.

He's not a liar. He has never lied about himself, which is why things have turned out like this. Another statement:

I am a man.

This should be a more straightforward statement than the last one, there is nothing obviously wrong with its logic. The problem with it is in the mirror. He unbuttons his shirt, trying not to avert his eyes.

There. Breasts. He has breasts, small but decidedly feminine in shape. This is what they've done to him. There was a man in ancient times called Tiresias, Alan learnt about him at school. He was also a paradox, he was a man with breasts, and he was a blind man who could see.

Alan can't remember what happened to Tiresias in the end but he knows it wasn't good. Seers never do end well, they are always punished for telling the truth. He doesn't know what will happen to himself. He has been told that the effect of the hormones will only last for as long as his criminal sentence, and then it will reverse itself. Until then, what? Will he have to live as this neutered creature; neither one thing nor the other?

He goes to the bedroom where the apple is waiting. There's a heavy, almost intoxicating scent of almonds in here. But it's too soon. The apple isn't perfect, it's got a small blemish like a birthmark. It's not a cartoon apple. He knows he's not in a cartoon but he's not sure if he's in reality.

He never thought he'd get trapped in his own test, imitating a woman. He wishes he hadn't predicted this, hadn't written down these theoretical ideas which have become real, like fairy stories coming to life.

The first version of his idea was this: a man and a machine

both pretend to be a woman and a judge has to decide who is better at the pretence; the machine or the man. The second version was simpler in a way; the machine has to pretend to be human, and the man doesn't have to do any pretending. The judge decides who is better at being human, the man or the machine.

He thinks he prefers the first version, perhaps because the ability to lie and pretend you're something other than yourself is the secret of human intelligence. The second test is more a test of human behaviour; no actual intelligence is required.

He walks away from the mirror towards the record player. It's not too late to put on a record and have a short dance. Perhaps he could get a job as one of those fairground freaks, half man and half woman. The male half with a little beard and semi-suit, stitched onto a scrap of a ball gown, worn by the female half. He has the cleavage now for a ball gown. He wraps his arms around himself and moves around the room to the music. Snow White's glass cover is a bit scratched now, but the inner workings are still visible.

Even after he started taking the hormones he tried to go out, to pubs. He even went abroad once, as he used to do regularly. In spite of the drugs he can still offer himself to men, in the way that a woman does. But it's no use, as predicted by the judge, other men are repulsed by him. There seems to be no space in the real world for the illogical statement that he now embodies.

He goes back to the bedroom, takes a bite from the apple and lies down on the bed. He shuts his eyes and waits for the prince to come.

The voice-activated lift

When my department moved into a new open-plan office, the managers asked me to work out the seating arrangements. I was given a large sheet of graph paper and I drew little boxes on it in a grid formation and wrote a name in each box. Each box was a desk and each name was a person. I thought it worked quite well, I'd even managed to allocate space for the pot plants as well as for 'breakout' areas with coffee machines to encourage the staff to relax. We were allowed to purchase sofas for these areas and by all accounts they've been highly successful. The plants are thriving.

My own desk happened to be next to the only window in the office. Unfortunately, although this was merely a coincidence, my colleagues noticed and they stopped speaking to me.

They never spoke to me very often anyway, so it hasn't made a lot of difference to my life. But I don't feel I can sit on the sofas, and people visit me only when they have to pass on some work.

My desk is quite near the lift, which is the first voice-activated one I have ever encountered. There are no buttons to press, just a small metal grill and when someone gets into the lift a voice comes out of the grill and says, 'Speak the number of the floor into this grill slowly and clearly. Zero is the number of the ground floor.'

Sometimes the lift's voice is the only one that speaks to me all day. The voice is female, nice and gentle-sounding, and I enjoy listening to her.

On the first day in the new office I tried out the lift. 'One,' I said and it worked. The journey was smooth, the lift's motion almost imperceptible.

I became curious about the lift's abilities so I decided to test it, 'Two. No, perhaps I mean three. I'm not sure.' But it managed to ignore my attempt to mislead it, it just picked out the essential information and delivered me to the correct floor.

The managers were pleased with my seating plan. But the next piece of work that they gave me is somewhat more demanding, I must write a report with a definition of outer space. I've been working on this for weeks, trying to understand the views of all the different experts. When I get stuck I'm able to stare out of my window at the city, at all its roofs and metal buildings with the sky above always busy with planes and clouds.

The managers and the Minister need to know where outer space is so they can regulate it. All I can say for certain is that outer space is a long way above this Government department. When I'm working on the report I can picture myself floating around freely up there, a long way away from all this ordinary stuff.

Monday morning and on the way to work I treat myself to a café latte with hazelnut syrup. When I get into the lift I feel like I don't really want to go to my desk yet, so I tell it, 'A half'. It starts to move and then slows to a halt in that secret no-man's land that always exists between floors. It stops there for precisely the same length of time that my colleagues used to spend politely laughing at one of my jokes, and then without either of us saying anything it delivers me to my own floor.

All day as I sit trying to work on the report I can see the lift out of the corner of my eye. Its doors open periodically to reveal its inner metallic space, and I can hear my colleagues telling it numbers in slow, solemn voices like children in primary school learning to count.

I still haven't finished the report although my managers are waiting for it, the Minister is waiting for it, everyone out there is waiting for it. But I don't know what it will say. None of the numbers make sense to me. I spend my day gazing at Excel spreadsheets, and when I'm not doing that I stare out of the window and try not to imagine things crashing out of the sky onto the people below.

Last month a Russian satellite fell to earth in the Outer Hebrides and every news site around the world had pictures of the remains of the dog walker (and his dog) being scraped up off the machair. After that there were calls for something to be done. Laws to be passed.

In order to regulate something, the Government has to know what it is or at least where it is. And nobody can agree on precisely where normal, everyday space stops and outer space starts. My report is supposed to make the definitive pronouncement, but each expert that's been consulted has a different opinion. So the report is still imaginary. I have a title for it, and headings for the different parts of it. I've even typed my name at the end of it. The rest of it is just blank white space.

At lunchtime I'm looking forward to escaping for a bit. Talking to the lift is the first time I've spoken today, so I test it again, 'One minus one.' My voice is a bit croaky from lack of use, but the lift doesn't hesitate. It's clearly able to do maths, and so it takes me to the ground floor.

That afternoon, there's another email from the managers. Parliament has been waiting for the report for so long that they suspect there's been some sort of cover-up, and they've summoned me to give evidence to the Outer Space Committee. I've never heard of this committee before, perhaps it's made up of politicians bobbing around in spacesuits.

When I was young, I saw '2001: A Space Odyssey' and I fantasised about being an astronaut. After that, whenever I felt lonely at school because the other children weren't talking to me, I'd imagine being all safe and snug inside my spacesuit and doing a walk outside my rocket, completely surrounded by space. That thin layer of the spacesuit would be the only barrier between me and infinity. But now I'm stuck because

I can't find the line that I always assumed was there. Perhaps there is no obvious barrier and it's more of a gentle thinning out of daylight and air to darkness and vacuum. Perhaps each astronaut must learn how to travel upwards through the prosaic clutter to beautiful emptiness.

I feel agitated by this summons to the committee, so I leave my desk and wander over to the breakout area. Even though we haven't been in this office longer than a few weeks I'm dismayed to see that the sofas have already acquired a layer of food stains and crumbs. They look thoroughly used. And when I return to my desk a few minutes later, I can tell that someone's disturbed it. The stack of papers has been ruffled, the array of biros is out of kilter, my coffee mug has been moved. I look around but everyone appears to be hard at work. No way of telling who has been here, disturbing my space.

I can't work anymore, I have to leave the office. In the lift I become calmer as I experience its slow but sure motion down through the building. I place my hand on the wall of the lift. It feels warm and it's vibrating slightly, making me think of a sleeping body curled up next to me in my bed. I'm capable of imagining such a thing.

The next day there is nothing on my desk. No paper or biros or in-tray, even my computer and keyboard have gone. All that's left is a smooth, flat surface to contemplate. Perhaps the managers have moved me to another office, or perhaps it's an extension of yesterday's disturbance. There's no way of telling. It's sort of restful, in a way, to sit at an empty desk when everyone around me is working.

But after a few minutes I get bored. I go over to the lift and I stand in the middle of it, not particularly near the grill, so that I have to speak in a loud voice and all of my colleagues can hear me, 'Pi.'

'Pi,' the lift's voice repeats softly.

Pi is the beautifully endless number that can never be completely known. Perhaps it's odd to stand in the metal cube of the lift and be reminded of pi, but there is something about the unreal voice in the lift that is better than any other voice I have had to listen to in my life.

The doors shut. I lean against the wall and feel the lift's tiny judder travel through my body as it tries to calculate my command. It creeps from approximation to approximation in search of mathematical perfection without once complaining. I know it will take an eternity to calculate pi. I can relax in here.

The competition for immortality

The fat man stayed squatting right in the middle and didn't ever move, while all around him the skinny people were rushing around so frantically that some of them bounced off the edges of the space. Their job was to bring the fat man biscuits which he ate quickly, spilling crumbs everywhere. The skinny people pecked at these crumbs which gave them more energy and so they rushed around even faster, and brought the fat man more biscuits and he distributed more crumbs.

In fact, the visual output of this program was actually quite crude, the skinny people weren't much more than lines of black pixels. The fat man was just a circle with a mouth, he didn't need limbs or eyes. The graphics weren't important, they weren't the essential part of the program because the real output was invisible, a database stored in the computer's memory.

But to make it more entertaining she'd managed to superimpose a photo of their boss's face onto the fat man, and all the lab-people were gathered around the screen and laughing because the program was a perfect analogy of life in the department. The 'biscuits': the academic papers, grant applications, conference proceedings, press releases and so on all had to be fed into the boss. And in return everybody else (the lab-people, the coders and the admin assistants) just got crumbs of grant money.

It felt odd watching her colleagues laugh at something she'd created, because she didn't interact with them much on a daily basis. Her office in the computing section at the top of the building always seemed too far away for the lab-people to reach from their home in the basement. She wasn't sure exactly what they all did down there, but she knew some of it involved cutting up brains with a machine that looked disturbingly like a bacon slicer.

So as a farewell present, and partly because her grant was due to run out and she'd be leaving this place soon, she'd adapted one of her codes and added in the boss's photo as an offering to the lab-people. And here they all were, gathered around a laptop amongst the workbenches and bottles of liquids and glass dishes and fridges and centrifuges and white coats and bits of nameless machinery. Down here she could smell a rich and complex perfume of chemicals. Sometimes this smell rose up past the entrance to the lab but it never made it beyond the first floor. The floor where she worked just smelt of old shoes.

This was what she did for a living, she created computer simulations in which virtual animals she called 'beasties' could move around and eat food. If the beasties ate too much food it would run out and they would starve, so their numbers seesawed up and down as they cycled through periods of feast and famine. The latest innovation that she'd added to the beasties' world was to give them another type of food, so they now had grass that needed to be cultivated and meat that needed to be hunted. But although there was plenty of food, the beasties' behaviour was rather chaotic and they didn't seem able to feed themselves very effectively. They moved in random directions, as if confused by what was on offer. She always pictured them as lumbering animals that worried about sudden loud noises or hidden predators. Even though there weren't any noises or any predators in the code, the beasties might have a whole hidden mental existence. After all, they did in her imagination.

And when she left this department, she was going to have to leave them behind. Even though she'd written the code that created the beasties, it was the intellectual property of the department. They weren't really hers. As the lab-people laughed at the pixellated biscuit-eating she felt a pang of nostalgia and she wondered how the beasties would cope. There was still one more variable that she wanted to introduce to their world before she left them for good.

The lab-man standing next to her by the laptop, who grinned at her sometimes when the boss was being excessively verbose in seminars, suggested they all go to the pub. She'd worked here nearly three years and only been invited to the pub a couple of times. So she ran to get her coat and when she found them again they were halfway down the street, with their arms linked like some long chained molecule. In the pub they shoved up to make space for her so she was able to settle down next to the man, and a few drinks later he spoke to her, 'Do you ever compare your computer simulations to the real world?'

'Other people do that.' The beer was slipping down smoothly and the man's hand was resting very near to hers on the sofa. She fancied she could feel the warmth of it.

'Have you ever looked through a microscope?' he asked. 'At real things?'

She shook her head, she didn't do microscopes.

'Come and have a look. I'll show you a whole new world.'

She said she'd think about it and then she fell quiet again, she wanted to listen to some more of the lab-people's talk because they were all so easy with each other, it made her feel comfortable too. They were talking now about the annual 'Fruit Fly Olympics' where different strains of fruit flies competed for the honour of being set free in the boss's office.

'Come and look tomorrow,' the man spoke to her more quietly and more insistently than before. Then his hand came down on top of hers as if they'd both planned it, and maybe they had.

Once, she had written a code about sexual reproduction and it didn't have any graphics because nobody but her needed to analyse the output, and anybody else who was interested in it could use their imagination. But later that night as the man was shedding some of his cells inside her, she ran a finger around the swirls of his ears, and she examined the colours of his eyelashes. She looked at the way his fingers were splayed out on the bed, as if he were trying to grasp something just out of reach. The more she examined him, the more complexity she could find. Perhaps that's what real life was, endless complexity and all of it beautiful.

The next morning it was raining so hard that when he took her hand and led her into the lab, water washed down the windows and it looked like they were walking under the sea. The air felt murky and textured and ripples of light swayed across the floor and the benches as he showed her the alcove where the microscope stood. 'This is Cyclops,' he told her.

'Cyclops?'

'It's only got one eye.' He stood behind her as she peered down the tube and she could tell he was smiling into the moist darkness of the room. But all she could see was the enlarged reflection of her own eye looking back up at her, the lashes grossly magnified, the pupil as black as ever. She tried for some time until she had to give up.

Later that morning she made the final planned change to the code. She introduced a genetic mutation that affected the speed of the beasties so that some of them could move quicker than others.

When the code was up and running, she continued to work on job applications for various labs and institutes around the world. She imagined her life branching out across a map, and wondered what would change and what would stay the same if she moved somewhere else. Then the code stopped, the beasties had all died unexpectedly early. She adjusted the parameters of the mutation and started the code again, trying not to think about how many beasties had died in total since she started work here.

The lab-man came upstairs to see her. She told him about

her work and showed him some earlier outputs of the code.

Later that night as he covered her breasts with his hands he said, 'Beastie.' She smiled, thinking he was trying to be funny, but he seemed unsettled by something.

'You don't know what they look like,' she whispered. Somehow the dark made it easier to say things.

'Yes I do.' He twisted into her, 'They look like you. You made them, didn't you?'

They stopped talking at that point but afterwards an idea came to her. As he lay sleeping she thought about it some more, until she'd figured out a way to do it.

She had to break into the lab. But there wasn't any broken glass on the floor or a figure prowling around with a stocking over her head. It was more mundane than that; all she had to do was make sure the lab-people were at the pub, then return and remember the access code for the door.

Down here the smell felt three-dimensional, both sharp and dank. In the corner a tap dripped as incessantly as a heartbeat and hollowed-out lab coats hung on the wall. The blinds were not entirely drawn shut so that moonlight made a barcode on the floor and walls.

But she ignored the coats and the stripes of light; she had a job to do. She'd watched the lab-people at work, so she went over to the incubators where the samples were kept, and opened one of the doors. A neat stack of flasks glinted at her. Now she set to work. She scraped her cheek with a wooden spatula, and sterilised what she'd collected so that her cells became decontaminated and pure. At this stage those cells were practically invisible and she could barely see them as she deposited them in a flask. She held the flask up to the window, imagining them growing and forming a thin film on the culture, before becoming more substantial and making their presence felt.

She wanted to work her way through all the flasks, but there were a lot of them and her cheeks became raw very quickly, so she had to consider other possibilities.

Together, she and the lab-man hadn't gone this far in the lab. The previous day there had been a surreptitious fumble, a half-hearted struggle against the firm grip of waistbands and bra straps, but not this gleam of naked skin in full moonlight or this parting of her legs in plain view of the workbenches. As she claimed her own cells from inside her, she pictured the brains stored nearby. Now the lab felt like an appropriate place for bodies to meet and touch, and assert themselves against their stripped-down, disassembled counterparts in the lab fridges.

Back in the pub she saw that the lab-man was talking to a lab-woman, his arm within touching distance of her shoulders. And she wondered why she had been so easy to forget.

After a bit the lab-man noticed her standing there, and slid his arm away from the other woman. He even smiled. 'Where'd you disappear to, Beastie?' he asked and he swallowed the last of his pint, the Adam's apple in his neck working hard.

'The lab,' she replied and he laughed. 'I want to go back there with you,' she told him. But he laughed again and the other woman joined in, so all she could do was pretend she'd made a joke, and wait for him to finish talking.

That night in bed she thought of what she'd done in the moonlit lab, until the audience of lab-coats trembled in her head. Afterwards, she realised the lab-man was watching her. 'In your own world, weren't you?' he said as he slid away from her.

The code was working as she hoped; the mutation that she'd introduced made the beasties move at different speeds, the slow ones cultivated the grass and the fast ones hunted the meat. They shared food with each other so that everyone got a varied diet. The program ran and ran and generations of beasties grew and ate, and she could imagine them sitting around their fires at night telling each other stories of famous hunts in the past. They probably wove necklaces with the longer stalks of grass and made musical instruments out of old bones.

There was a rumour. Something was happening downstairs in the lab, something unexpected was going on with the new cultures. Tests were being carried out but the lab-people were confused and her boss was worried. When she hurried past his office one morning she could hear him shouting down the phone, the cultures were behaving oddly and he wanted to know the reason why. In the sanctity of her own office she doodled, and analysed the beasties' activities.

Later that day she emailed the lab-man. She hadn't seen him for a few days and so they arranged to meet after work in the carpark. Usually, as he left the lab, the lab-man was whistling but today there was just silence. She suggested that they go for a drink but he didn't seem keen. He wanted to go back to work and figure out what was happening with the cultures.

It was cold outside, the cars were losing their colour in the twilight, and she felt that if she stood here for much longer she would become part of this shadowy half-world. Other people were leaving the building and she watched them hurry away as if eager to abandon their earlier daytime selves.

She tried to start another conversation but her words just dwindled into the air.

'I'm sorry,' he said, 'I don't have time for this.' He walked away, and after a few seconds she couldn't see him anymore. She guessed he'd disappeared back into the building.

She stood there for a bit longer before she also went back inside, because she couldn't think of anything else to do. In her office, yet another job offer popped into her in-box, her fourth. Around her, the possibilities of her future lives flickered but she found it difficult to believe in any of them now. They seemed more virtual than the beasties.

Many floors below her, she knew the lab-man would be looking down the microscope at her cells, growing and dividing. His eye staring right at her without knowing what she ever was.

Heroes and cowards

If this is a proper story written down in a book, then I myself most likely would not be the hero of it. I would be the narrator, the man on the outside watching the events. But whatever kind of story it is, it started that morning in the café and it came after the end of a much larger story, one which I took part in and which has been written about elsewhere. Well, most of it anyway.

I'm sitting in the café trying to work out how long I can afford to stay in LA before having to go back east to my home town, and I'm wondering what's happened to my life since I got demobbed. I got the suit, I got a job and then another job, but nothing's stuck to me. At least not the things I want; money, a girl, a decent place to live. Or perhaps I just think I want them. Why don't I give up and go home? But that feels like the wrong direction, I want to stay here in a city where so many things are still unknown to me and waiting to be found.

It's raining. I didn't think it was supposed to rain in LA. But I stir my coffee and look at the rain and wonder what to do with the rest of my life. I wasn't expecting to get this far.

I've got my 'gimme a job' smile – I practise it each morning when I shave, but it's not a good smile. It's like a dog, trying to get you to like him. I know it makes people want to kick me. Hell, *I* want to kick me.

Still, I feel as fresh as a peeled egg as I sit in that café checking the situations vacant column in the newspaper, so engrossed that at first I don't notice the other man. And it's only when he clears his throat that I look up and realise he's waiting for me to notice him before he speaks to me. He's polite like that. He's always polite.

'Looking for work?'

I smile. He can see me reading the paper. 'You too?'

He shakes his head, 'Not me, no. I'm fixed up.'

'Well, good for you,' and I'm about to go back to my paper when he sits forward.

'Stan.' I should be surprised that he know my name, but somehow I'm not. He opens his matchbook and I see the clean rows inside, 'How many job interviews you had, Stan?'

I don't reply. I've got my pride.

'You've enough money for eight more days before you're on that train back home to Milwaukee. That's the case, isn't it?'

He's done the math better than I can. I nod. I wonder if it's going to rain for those eight days and then rain some more when I get home. I want him to put the matches away, but he just flicks one of them with his thumbnail before continuing, 'I saw you this morning in your bathroom, shaving in front of the mirror. Nice the way you've set it up so the mirror's opposite the window. To catch the light, I suppose. Makes it easy for us.'

Us. Who is he? Who are they? I fold my paper into quarters and make a neat cross with my pencil next to one of the adverts without reading it.

'Back home to your family. Your family's originally from Germany, isn't that right?'

He has the quietest voice. I have to lean forward to hear him properly, and the whole time he speaks, his mouth barely moves.

I pull down the sleeves of my suit as far as they go, 'It was a long time ago, way before –'

'Of course, of course.' His voice goes even softer.

'It's the Commies now, I thought –'

'Yes Stan, it is the Commies now.'

The waitress pours me some more coffee. During the week that I've been coming to this café, it's always been the same waitress with the same smile. I wonder if she peels it off and stashes it away with her nylons each night. I wonder if she's waiting for something, too, the same way I am.

The man waits until she's gone before continuing, 'You speak German, Stan?'

I nod again, even more confused, 'A little, with my folks. My dad, he's not so hot at English.'

'That's going to be very useful.'

'Useful? For what?'

And that's how they get me. What choice do I have? They're right, after all. I do only have enough money for eight more days before I have to get on a train and head back home to that dump of a town near Milwaukee. So I take it. It's not so bad. It's not all hanging round on street corners. Well some of it is. And the other guys, they're alright. They'll stand you a coffee.

They give me this job. I have to follow some German guy and get information about him for a committee hearing the Government is organising. I never heard of him before but they said I'm ideal for it. I ask them what information I'm supposed to be getting, but they're vague. Anything, they said. Anything at all. The guy writes stuff for the movies, and his name is Brecht.

Brecht and Laughton decide to have a break from working and Brecht goes into his little kitchen to make tea for them both. They've been working hard, translating and updating Brecht's play 'Galileo' into English in time for its run at the Coronet Theatre which will start in a few weeks. Laughton will play the title role.

They do not speak each other's language very well, so work is slow and not terribly efficient. In spite of this they talk a lot to each other as they work. Everything depends on the words, according to Laughton. Brecht is not so sure, the physical gesture is just as important.

While he waits for the tea, Laughton puts on a record of 'Die Dreigroschenoper' and sings along to it.

'For Heaven's sakes, stop that noise!' Brecht bellows from the kitchen.

'Why? It's one of your own, I thought you'd like it. A bit of your past.'

'The way *you* sing does not remind me of my past, it just gives me a headache. And we need to make progress.' Brecht appears in the living room with two small glasses of black tea.

'Black again?' Laughton mutters almost under his breath, 'can't we ever have milk in our tea?'

'Disgusting English habit,' Brecht sets the glasses down on the low coffee table, 'and we cannot even agree about the ending to the play.'

Laughton wanders over to the window of the study and looks out at the garden, 'Perhaps we'd do better working outside. A bit of fresh air and sunshine to stimulate our brains.'

Brecht purses his lips, 'Surely it would distract you, dear Charles.'

Laughton remains at the window, with his back to Brecht, 'I never get fed up with the weather here. If you'd come from where I came from, you'd feel a thrill every time you saw the sun and the turquoise sea, and all these flowers and pretty girls in skimpy clothes...'

'I thought you preferred staring at pretty boys.'

Laughton peers nervously around the room as if his wife is hiding there, 'Ssh.'

'I thought Elsa liked pretty boys too. I thought it was something the two of you had in common. Anyway, how is Elsa? We haven't seen her lately.'

Laughton pauses before answering, 'I think she's fine.'

'Why don't you both come over to dinner tonight?' Brecht spreads out his hands, 'Helene will make some of her terrific dumplings and we can all imagine we are somewhere civilised.'

'We're usually busy in the evenings. Elsa goes out a lot. But thank you anyway.'

They sip their tea. Laughton is obviously trying not to wince at the bitterness and Brecht smiles to himself.

'I think we should work at my house tomorrow,' Laughton announces as he sets down his empty glass, 'there is so much more space. And we have all the dictionaries there.'

Brecht shrugs. Laughton clearly needs his milk and sugar. And his boys. And maybe even his wife.

Laughton clambers out of the rickety armchair that made it to Los Angeles from Germany with Brecht and Helene, and stands as if he is on stage addressing an audience, 'Alright, alright, let's get on with it. The end of the play. We're going to let the audience feel some sympathy for Galileo? After all, he's old and broken, and up in front of the Inquisition.'

'Sympathy destroys what we are trying to achieve, Charles. When those Nazi gangsters started snivelling at their trials in Nürnberg, did you feel sympathy?'

Laughton looks shocked, 'Of course not. It's hardly the same thing. But you've made the old man look like a coward.'

'Perhaps it's better to be a coward than a hero.' As usual, Brecht has an answer for everything and he can't resist replying to Laughton. 'Cowards generally live while heroes die. But he should have spoken up for science and not given in. Those scientists who built the Bomb, they did exactly what Galileo did; they obeyed the authorities. Except this time, it's even worse.'

The theatre is about half full, the audience scattered throughout the auditorium. Brecht peeps out at them through a hole in the curtain, from his position in the wings. Laughton is on stage and the play is coming to its end.

'*I taught you science and I denied the truth.*' As he speaks the lines, Laughton is bent over, his body remarkably twisted. The audience can believe that this is an old, blind man.

'Very good,' murmurs Brecht. 'Show the old man's self-loathing.'

'Science's sole aim must be to lighten the burden of human existence. If the scientists, brought to heel by self-interested rulers, limit themselves to piling up knowledge for knowledge's sake, then science can be crippled and your new machines will lead to nothing but new impositions.'

One man in the audience has become increasingly agitated throughout the performance, writhing around in his seat and muttering under his breath, and the other audience members are glaring at him. Brecht has been watching him with amusement, hoping that he will eventually react. He doesn't disappoint.

'Nonsense!' he finally cries out, but he seems ashamed of himself after this outburst and sinks back down into his seat. A man sitting behind him taps him on the shoulder.

'Make them remember the horror, Charles. The horror of the Bombs.' Brecht clenches the curtain.

'As a scientist I had a unique opportunity. If one man had put up a fight it might have had tremendous repercussions. Had I stood firm the scientists could have developed something like the doctors' Hippocratic Oath. As things are, the best that can be hoped for is a race of inventive dwarfs who can be hired for any purpose.'

'Nonsense!' the man in the audience cries out again. His face has gone red, which pleases Brecht. Their words have made this man think. He'll remember this night out at the theatre.

When the play is over, Brecht goes to the front of house to watch the audience coming out into the cool night air, and lights a cigar. He wants to see their faces, to see if they've understood what he's been trying to say. It's mostly students who come to this theatre. Where are the workers in this town? The dockers? The street sweepers? The farmhands who pick the lemons in the vast orchards? He is not sure who his people are here, apart from the other exiled German writers, huddled together in smart bungalows at the top of one of the canyons.

Groups of girls wander past and he smiles absent-mindedly

at them. A young man hangs around the foyer watching them and furtively making notes with a pencil he keeps having to lick. He seems to be watching Brecht too. Perhaps he is a – Brecht gropes for the word – a spook?

Then – 'How dare you!'

'Excuse me?'

It is the agitated man, the man who shouted out. Brecht wants to thank him for his participation, his reaction, but the man is still clearly agitated. Indeed, he is angry.

'"A race of inventive dwarfs?" Is that it? Is that your verdict on scientists? On the whole of science?'

'Excuse me? Who are you? What is your profession?' Brecht would really like to know the type of person who is interested in this play.

'I'm one of your dwarfs. And I can punch pretty hard for a dwarf!' He swings at Brecht and makes contact with his jaw. Brecht stumbles backwards and his cigar goes flying.

'Ah, so you are a scientist,' he feels his jaw while he speaks. Painful, but not broken. Worse has happened to him, usually but not always, as a result of women. The rest of the audience has disappeared, hardly anyone else has noticed this audience member shouting at, and then hitting, a small man dressed in an odd, foreign-looking leather coat.

'Damn right I am! I worked on the Manhattan Project!' The man is jabbing his finger at Brecht but does not look like he will hit him again. Brecht can usually judge these things fairly well. The first punch took him by surprise though, he'll admit that.

'Ah... then you know what I am talking about in this play. Selling your soul and so on.'

'I know what *you're* talking about. But do you know what *scientists* talk about? Night and day we worked to develop the Bomb, because we thought it would save lives! That's what *we* talked about. Hell, the war would still be going *now* if it wasn't for the Bomb!' The man seems to find it easier to express himself, now that he's no longer confined to being part of the audience.

'I am glad you had such interesting discussions whilst you prostituted yourselves to the authorities and worked to destroy thousands of people. It must make you feel so much better now, the memories of those discussions.'

'I tell you what makes me feel better, and that's the thought of my fist hitting your face!' Perhaps Brecht has not judged this right after all, because the man looks murderous. Where is Charles, for heaven's sakes? Charles wouldn't be able to hit anyone but he is at least a big man. He appears imposing.

A young woman hurries over, 'Leave Mr Brecht alone!'

'Leave *me* alone, you mad woman!' Although she is a small girl, she clearly knows how to slap a man. Brecht smiles gratefully at her as the scientist sidles out of the building, muttering to himself. Time to find Charles, and have a celebratory drink.

'Mr Brecht!' the woman follows him, 'please wait! Can I talk to you for a moment?'

Brecht sighs. He would like to drink a large brandy. But the woman really is very pretty. Slim, dark, oriental. He smiles at her again.

Brecht is meeting Laughton at his house. Even though the play has already opened, they still want to work on it. Particularly the ending. The troublesome ending.

Laughton is in his garden, wearing shorts and trimming some sort of flowering plant. Brecht doesn't know the name for it in German, never mind in English. And it is pointless to learn, now. He does not feel terribly motivated to learn more English words.

Laughton grins at him, 'Pretty good, Bertie boy.'

'Pretty good, Charles.' But he doesn't grin back. May as well get to the point, 'Why do you keep playing it differently to the way I tell you to?'

Laughton pauses, shears hanging from one hand, 'Because you're not actually the director, Bertie, even though you like to tell everyone what to do. You're not even an actor. You're just the writer, and here in Hollywood that doesn't count for much.' There is an edge of steel in his voice that hasn't been there in their previous discussions and rehearsals.

'But you didn't speak the line where Galileo acknowledges he was not in any real danger!'

'It's better without it. If Galileo genuinely thinks he's under threat of the Inquisition's torture instruments, then it makes it more dramatic. He's a more interesting person, more three-dimensional. You want to make it all black and white but there's no point in acting such a cardboard character, the audience would get bored and so would I. I thought you wanted to educate people through theatre, but if you just shout at them and hector them, they'll fall sleep. You've got to be more subtle.'

Brecht is taken aback. 'I thought we wanted people to realise that what he did was wrong. And it's something people should be thinking about *now*. Did you know Oppenheimer is about to be given some sort of award for his work on the Bomb?'

'Galileo and Oppenheimer don't have anything in common, Bertie. Galileo underwent a show trial and made a forced confession. Oppenheimer *chose* to do what he did.' Laughton snips off a dead rose. Brecht cannot tell what colour it once was before it falls into the long grass and is lost.

'Galileo was the first modern scientist. There is a direct link between him and Oppenheimer. He had a unique opportunity to stand up for truth.'

'You're just like a scientist yourself! You set up your little experiment, you get people to watch it and you expect them to think what you think. But proper scientists are open minded about the results and I think you've tried to rig your experiment.'

'Rig? Like a lighting rig?'

Laughton sighs, 'Not quite, Bertie boy. Not quite.'

I'm back in the same café, trying not to stare at the legs of the same waitress.

It's just across the street from my apartment. The first time I came here, I thought it was a fancy neighbourhood because the fronts of the buildings on the street are magnificent, all painted and carved wood. But the actual buildings crouch behind them as if ashamed to be seen. And all I have is a room with a hotplate and a shared bathroom down the corridor. I heat up frankfurters on the hotplate and eat them standing at the window looking out at the scenery. There's not much else to look at in the room itself. From where I stand I can see a little bit of ocean, about the size of my thumbnail. It's funny to think that this is the same ocean we fought in, thousands of miles away. The same water slopping over dead bodies.

A girl enters the café, slim, dark, Oriental. She's clutching a pile of books to her chest and looking around for a place to sit. There's a free chair opposite me.

'Mind if I –' she says, but it's just for show and she sinks into it before I can reply. I sip my coffee and try not to look at her. She's too pretty to look at directly. She's one of those girls you have to take sideways glances at, in case you get burned, so I can only catch glimpses of her straight black hair, and delicate pink lips.

She's perusing the menu, and I'm making my coffee last longer than it normally does. I should be out of there, tailing Brecht.

The waitress appears, 'What'll it be?'

'One egg sunny side up and a rasher of bacon, and hash fries, and a link sausage. Oh, and two pieces of toast. White, with jelly. No butter.' She's got a big appetite for such a little girl, and for some reason that cheers me up. The waitress cocks an eyebrow at me.

'Just a refill of coffee. Please.'

After the waitress has gone I say to the girl, 'I've seen you before.'

She sighs and looks out the window, so I have the opportunity to see her profile.

'No, no, I really have,' I think about it for a moment. 'At the theatre,' I say finally, 'you were the girl who slapped that man.'

She lays her hands flat on the table, which is still sticky from having been wiped by the waitress and grins at me, 'He deserved it!'

'Do you often hit men?' I try to make it sound funny and flirtatious but she takes me seriously.

'I hit him because he hadn't listened to the play. He'd actually worked on the Bomb!'

'So that's where you're from? Japan.'

I can't keep that note from my voice, the hard note. And this is clearly the wrong thing to ask her, because her voice is also hard now, 'I was born here.'

'Ok, you got me,' after all I wasn't born here, and so I spread my hands out and smile my loser's smile at her. But she doesn't smile back which is a pity because I want her to, I want to see her face tipped up to mine, breathless, waiting. I watch an awful lot of bad movies. Perhaps that's the only way I can understand the world around me, in terms of scenery and acting, and false words and looks.

She does at least carry on talking to me, 'Anyway he started it. He was going for Mr Brecht!'

'Brecht? You know him?'

'Of course I know him! He's a famous playwright!' I am being told off by a butterfly, a lotus flower.

'Yeah, but do you actually know him?'

She narrows her eyes, 'Why? Why are you interested?'

Why indeed. I am not very good at this job. I am too obvious, too straightforward, I can't hide what I want. This is why I never get the girl, or the information.

'I'm trying to interview him. For a paper back East.'

'You're a journalist? Which paper?' Her cutlery is paused over her breakfast. Some things I am good at in my job. Like noticing the physical stuff. The way the yolk shines innocently in the sunlight before it gets all torn apart.

'Just a small one. You won't have heard of it.'

'A small paper back East sent you all the way here just to interview Mr Brecht? Must be an awfully intellectual paper,' but she is smiling again and my heart leaps and soars. I can do it this time.

'My name's Stan,' I say.

'Stan. I'm Hiroko. Maybe we should join forces. I'm trying to get an interview with Mr Brecht too. For my college newspaper.'

She holds out her hand, and I am allowed to touch it.

'My, you've got clean hands for a journalist. Usually they're all inky and dirty,' and she laughs at me. I laugh back. I will need to buy some ink if I'm going to see her again.

And I do see her again. We meet over breakfast and eat toast together and she tells me she's interested in 'Mr' Brecht because of his politics. He is an inspiration to workers everywhere, apparently. She asks me for tips on interviewing him. I used to interview people when I was in the army, but that's probably not the sort of interviewing she means. Finally, I risk asking her for a date.

'A date?' She pokes her knife into some left-over jelly. She doesn't look at me, 'Sure. Ok. A date.' The word 'date' sounds foreign when she says it.

I wonder what she is thinking, 'Tomorrow? Are you free tomorrow?'

She nods, 'Of course I'm free.'

'Meet you in front of the Ritzy at seven.' I try not to sound triumphant.

'Are you going to bring me a corsage?' She laughs a little.

'Maybe.' But I don't laugh. I will bring her anything she wants.

Brecht receives a letter. He doesn't receive many letters here, people tend to use the telephone. This letter looks official and he has the old fear that they have found out some secret of his and they will require him to leave. He doesn't feel protected here in this country, living in a city where earthquakes may strike at any moment, where landslides cause parts of people's gardens to fall off and into the sea below. This happened in Laughton's garden just last week and he lost a much-loved oak tree as a result.

Brecht carries the unopened letter through to the dining room, where Helene is sitting and drinking her morning coffee. She watches as he slits it open. She doesn't get many letters either.

Silence for several minutes.

'I have been subpoenaed,' Brecht says finally, 'to give evidence at their hearing.'

'Hearing? What hearing?' She pauses, her coffee cup halfway to her mouth. Helene likes her coffee, and most of it in this country is too weak. So she has to brew her own thick, dark, pungent liquid and the smell of it competes with Brecht's cigars in their small house.

'Their show trials. Their purges. No,' he corrects himself, 'no-one will be shot in the head or sent to a camp. They will just be publicly condemned. And not be able to work again.'

'For what?' Her voice is calm, unbothered. She is used to Brecht's outbursts against life here.

'For being a Communist. Which is apparently un-American. Or possibly even a Socialist. I'm not sure they understand the distinction.'

'Ah.' She does not react to this, but opens a newspaper lying next to her coffee and starts to read.

'Do you know what this means?' Brecht can't stop himself from sounding annoyed. Helene's calmness in the face of all their crises, such as having to leave Germany, then Denmark, then Sweden, is admirable. But sometimes he would like a reaction, a little drama. 'It means the end of us here.'

'Why? Can't you just refuse to do it? This is, supposedly, a democracy. People here have rights against the State. Even German playwrights have some rights. Say no.'

The castle walls rustle in the breeze, as Brecht and Laughton wander around. A tear in the fabric of the mad scientist's house exposes its cardboard frame. The colours, too, are not what Brecht imagined. The castle is painted purple, the house red and somewhat splotchy around the edges. It seems that film sets are even more fake than stage sets.

There is the constant sound of workmen hammering, presumably constructing a new set somewhere else. Brecht wonders if God views his work like this. A gigantic, or perhaps a very small, film set.

'You have to appear,' Laughton's face looks almost grey with worry. 'They will stop you working if you don't show up.'

'I don't *have* to do anything, dear Charles. Anyway, there is a whole group of us, nineteen people in fact, who will refuse. We will become *causes célèbres*.' He can see the newspaper headlines, the photos of their heroic faces. The workers who stood up to the State.

'Really?' Laughton doesn't look persuaded. They amble past a heap of wooden boards lying on the ground. The boards have clearly been there for some time, paint is peeling away from the surface, and the grain of the wood has been cracked apart by the heat of the sun.

'I wonder what that used to be,' says Brecht. Laughton is a good man, but perhaps he is the wrong man to speak to about such matters. Brecht cannot imagine him being outspoken about his own beliefs or actions.

Laughton smiles for the first time since they arrived at the studios, 'It amazes me how these film sets look so fake when you see them in real life, and yet on the screen they always convince.'

'Because the audience wants to believe what it is being shown.' Brecht can never resist the opportunity to make a point, 'That is what I hate about the movies. The audience should make up their own minds. But Frankenstein is still wonderful. I will never forget the mad scientist pulling the switch. The whole audience screamed when the monster started moving. And when it offered flowers to the child, I cried, Charles, I admit. I hated it, the shameless manipulation of my emotions. It made me angry, but I still cried. That's when I thought that it is wrong to make an audience feel emotions that are not real.'

'Emotions are always real, surely?' Laughton looks anxious again.

'You were not at the Nürnberg rallies. The manufacturing of extreme emotions out of air. Nobody had those emotions before Hitler conjured them up. And he learnt it from the movies, you know. It was more terrifying than anything, even Frankenstein. That's why I want my audiences to think, not to feel.'

'You can't stop people feeling, and empathising with other people.'

'Well, alright. But they must think too. And remain clear-headed, even when crying at the monster.' Brecht remembers sitting next to Helene as they watched the Frankenstein film in Berlin, and is suddenly overwhelmed by nostalgia. Why can't he be there, in the dusty cinema off Schönhauser Allee? Why does he have to be here in a city so full of film sets and flimflam and fake emotions that nobody can tell what is real anymore? His eyes fill.

'Aren't you feeling well?' asks Laughton.

'Dear Charles!' Brecht places a hand on his arm, 'I was just thinking about Elsa in that film. Who could ever forget her performance as the monster's bride? The most terrifying hairstyle ever seen in the movies.'

I'm due to meet Walter. We've arranged to meet on a street corner like proper spooks, and when I get there he's wearing this long mac and pulled his hat down low over his face, so that he looks a bit like a coat stand propped up against the wall.

'Any news on Brecht since your last report?' He starts to pick dirt out from under his fingernails with one of his matches.

'He's still working on that play with Laughton,' I try not to sound bored. I guess that's why Walter arranged to meet me here, to add a bit of excitement to the whole affair. Following people is boring, but I know it beats the hell out of any other possibilities available to me so I hold my tongue.

'You've been able to follow them? Every day?'

'Sure. Apart from one day. They went to a studio.'

'Never mind that. You told me Brecht is talking to someone about some music?'

'Yeah, Eisler. He's written a song for the play.'

'Do they talk about anything else?'

'No. Well, sometimes, they reminisce about Berlin. I guess it's their equivalent of the good old days.'

'Do they talk about Eisler's brother?'

'His brother? No I don't think so. What's his name?'

'Gerhard. Let me know if they do.'

'Right.' I stifle a yawn.

He glances at me from underneath the brim of his hat, 'You heard about this ceremony at Pasadena campus next week? To give Oppenheimer an award for the Bomb.'

'Yeah?' As far as I'm concerned Oppenheimer can have every award going for dropping the Bomb on Japan and stopping the war. Should have blown up the whole damn country, not just two cities.

'You know about the demonstration that's been planned to disrupt it?'

'No.'

'Really? I'm surprised. It's your little friend who's organising it. Seems she's quite a ringleader. As soon as you told us about her wanting to see Brecht, we looked her up. Interesting, very interesting.'

'You want me to – stop seeing her?'

'Stan… of course not. She's your friend. And she could be a very useful friend. So, when you meet her tonight and try and charm your way into her panties, just make sure and ask her about this demonstration. We want to know what she's planned. Otherwise, she may find herself helping us with our enquiries. And buy her a gardenia. She'll like that.'

He walks off at this point, leaving me just standing there, thinking about too much and not looking at what's right in front of my nose, so that a fat woman carrying a lot of bags collides with me and curses under her breath.

'Ma'am,' I tip my hat at her before walking away in the opposite direction to Walter. That's the way I've been taught by him and there's no doubt he's instructed me well. That's why I told Walter about meeting Hiroko because it seemed relevant to the job. But I didn't tell him everything, so how did he know about our date?

I walk along this street, impatient to get home and prepare for the evening, but the façades of LA are endless and I am walking for a long time.

Helene is always so calm, thinks Brecht, but she has nothing to do here. Hardly anyone knows her for what she really is. She does not fit in with the girls who sip sugary drinks in the diners on Wilshire Boulevard, waiting to be discovered and transformed into starlets. She is so calm because she has faced it all, the murder of her relatives, the imposition of being an exile over and over again in too many countries. And lastly, the baby. His but not hers. She was admirable about that. He can never look down on her, or even scale her heights. She is a mountain of a woman and he is nothing without her.

But he needs more. Charles is good but he needs the collaborators he used to have, Margarete, Elisabeth, Ruth. People who think in his own language so he is not constantly trying to reinvent himself in new words, which is exhausting.

He has the newspapers spread out in front of him, and he is searching through them. It is news, after all, a world premiere of a play by Brecht. 'Brecht' this time is himself and Laughton. In the past, 'Brecht' has been Brecht and Hauptmann, or Brecht and Berlau, or Brecht and Steffin. Or even Hauptmann and Brecht. She may have contributed more than him, on occasion.

Perhaps he should take Helene home. He is surprised by this thought and stops, the papers forgotten. Home. Where is home? Where there is work. Proper work for the two of them, and for others as well. It doesn't matter if he gets blacklisted here, he can't work properly in this place anyway.

Nothing happens for a long moment as he allows himself to dream about a workers' theatre in Germany. Then he goes back to the papers.

But the reviews confuse him. In spite of all his long speeches, they persist in seeing Galileo as a hero who defies the authorities by sacrificing his health to his work and smuggling that work out of the country under the noses of the Inquisition.

He sighs. A quote from one of the reviews snags in his mind, 'Condemn Galileo? I can't. Not when I see him on stage. On paper, it's another matter. But the words are nothing without the performance, the physical gestures. Only then can we understand the man.'

Hiroko's already waiting for me outside the Ritzy.

'Gardenias! My favourite! How did you know?' She looks happy.

'A lucky guess,' I grin. I don't care what happens after this evening, at least I've got her to myself for a few hours.

'So what's the movie? What are we going to see?'

'The Bachelor and the Bobby-Soxer', with Shirley Temple and Cary Grant.'

'You have to be joking.' She sounds incredulous and I don't blame her. With her charcoal hair and sad, sad eyes, she's about a million miles from being some vacuous blond bobby-soxer.

'No! It'll be great. Just pretend you're back at high school and you're on a date with the boy you had a crush on. The rest of the audience look like they're high-school kids anyway,' I try not to look too obviously at the audience around us. I can't see any of Walter's other men, but who knows? Perhaps they're just better at the job than I am.

'I never went on dates when I was a teenager. There weren't opportunities for dates at the place where I went to school,' and I see her hand is shaking slightly as she tries to pin the flower onto her dark dress. 'Could you do this for me, please?'

And so I get to feel the warmth of her body through the thin ash-grey fabric and I allow my hand to rest just a moment above her breast. The flower looks wrong now, almost garish against her monochrome beauty, but she looks down at it and smiles. Then she takes my hand and raises it to her mouth and she kisses it, 'Do we have to see the film?' she murmurs.

The feeling of her lips against my skin is the most intimate thing that has ever happened to me, far more moving than any hump I've had with some girl who only put out to get something back, like a pair of nylons or a good steak. I want to take Hiroko somewhere private but my room is too shabby and mean for her and I am ashamed of it, and she has to share a room with two other students. So we end up in the café again. At least we can talk there. But we will have to talk quietly so nobody can overhear us.

'What are you doing this Saturday?' She is sitting next to me, feeding me teaspoons of hot chocolate. The whole length of my arm is lying on the back of her chair, so that she can lean against it. I can take her weight, there is nothing to her, I think. I could hold her up.

'Saturday?' I have momentarily forgotten about Saturday.

'Yeah! Some friends of mine are going to this award ceremony for Oppenheimer. On the campus. You've heard about it?'

'Mm...' Now I don't want to think about Saturday and about Walter. Life should just be about beautiful Hiroko and hot chocolate.

'I'm planning a demonstration against it. It's outrageous! He shouldn't be given a medal, he should be put in jail for committing murder! A bunch of us are going to wave placards. You want to join us?' She sits up straight, making a gap between her and my arm, so I nod and she leans back against me again.

'You're just waving placards? Nothing else?'

'What else should there be? Riots? Bombs?' She laughs.

No, not bombs. No more bombs. I rest my face on her hair and breathe in deeply.

'Now Charles, I need you to help me.' In Laughton's garden again. The play has finished its run at the Coronet Theatre and will soon transfer to New York. Laughton is using the time off to tidy up the garden at the end of summer. Today he is raking leaves on the lawn.

'Ask away, dear boy,' Laughton is in one of his expansive moods. For a large man he can move quickly, and Brecht is sweating as he tries to keep up with him.

'I need to rehearse what I am going to say to this HUAC committee. I must give a perfect performance.'

Laughton stops raking and turns to him, 'I thought you weren't going to do it? I thought you'd refused, along with the rest of the nineteen?'

'I have changed my mind,' Brecht pauses and strikes a match to light the next cigar, but the sea breeze blows it out immediately, 'this appearance could be an opportunity, not a threat.'

'How?' Laughton lets the rake fall to the ground.

Brecht is so delighted by his thoughts that he seizes Laughton's hand, 'Because I can make it a performance! I can say the words in such a way as to make a mockery of the whole process!'

'Really?' Laughton looks extremely doubtful. 'Will they understand what you're doing? And if they do, isn't that even more dangerous than not appearing? Won't they clap you in prison for contempt of court?'

'No.'

'No?'

His cigar is properly lit now, and he breathes in. Laughton takes a step back away from the smoke. 'No, Charles. They will not have the opportunity to prepare a case against me and arrest me, because after I give my evidence I will leave this country!'

But this dramatic speech falls flat because Laughton simply stands and looks at him. Sometimes Brecht can't help thinking that they resemble Laurel and Hardy, Laughton's big round features and fleshy belly (he has even written an ode to Laughton's belly) contrasted with his own concave appearance and thin face.

'You're leaving before the New York run?' Laughton says.

'Yes. A small sacrifice I must make.'

'Oh, *you're* making the sacrifice, are you? Nobody else?'

'You'll be fine without me. You know what you're doing, now.'

'Glad you admit it, finally,' Laughton mutters as he picks

up the rake, and Brecht realises for the first time what a formidable weapon it could make.

'Charles, it was precisely your performance that made me realise what I can do at HUAC to undermine it! The way you constantly add more to my – to *our* words through your acting and gestures, you have rounded out Galileo from words to deeds.'

Laughton smiles, a bit thinly. 'Have you checked this out with your lawyers?'

A pause. 'Well, the lawyers have advised me to appear anyway. It seems I may not be protected by the Constitution.'

'Ah, so there is more than one motivation for this action,' but to Brecht's relief, Laughton continues to smile.

'And I must be extremely careful in the meantime before the hearing. So that is why I am going to have to turn down that very lovely and very persistent Japanese girl who keeps asking me to attend her demonstration against Oppenheimer. Besides, I am afraid Helene would be jealous if I said yes.'

'I thought you two didn't get jealous… and wasn't Helene the "other woman" once?' Laughton leans on his rake.

'Exactly, that's why she is worried. But I am too old now and I already have too many children to provide for. You are lucky, your extra-marital activities will never produce any children.'

'That's the only luck in it as far as I can see,' Laughton starts to rake again, but slower now. They don't speak for some time as Brecht watches him work.

'Charles, why don't you come to Germany with us? You know these activities used to be quite well tolerated there, at least in Berlin. I'm sure they will be again, soon.'

'Don't be absurd, Bertie. And besides, I like my routines here. I'm used to them.'

'But it's all so fake. You and your… friends, you're all married.'

'Well we are actors, after all. How do you know we don't mind being fakes in our private lives too?'

On Saturday the sun is so sharp it makes the campus look like a film set. White wooden chairs are set out in rows on the green grass facing a podium decked in red, white and blue ribbons. To one side a brass band are slowly assembling and tuning their shiny instruments. The audience are taking their seats, they look like the sort of people who would come to college award ceremonies and degree ceremonies. Not that I have ever been to either.

But I am thinking it all looks rather nice and am almost forgetting why I am here when Hiroko rushes up to me. For some reason she is wearing a raincoat and when she kisses me I can feel something sharp and angular press against me and intrude on our intimacy. She opens one button of the coat as if doing a striptease, so I can see the corner of a cardboard sign. For the demonstration, and my heart sinks. I scan the crowd but I can't see anyone obvious from the bureau. I never can.

She gestures behind her, 'The others,' she whispers theatrically. They look like typical students to me, round faces, shiny hair, shiny teeth. It's amazing to me that so soon after the war has finished there are already young kids like these, who've seen nothing, and who don't know what it all comes to, in the end.

We take our seats near the back and wait. One of the students giggles and Hiroko puts a finger to her lips, 'Sshhh!' I stroke her arm. It's quivering slightly, the way a bird quivers when you trap it in your cupped hands. 'Remember, we're going to be silent. This is a dignified protest, on behalf of the victims of the nuclear bombs who will never speak again.' She looks so dignified herself as she whispers these instructions to us, so dignified and serious. My Hiroko.

Things are beginning to happen. A rather tubby man climbs onto the stage, followed by Oppenheimer who's so slight that he's barely more than a dark crease in the air. He's wearing sunglasses as well as his trademark hat, the one that's in all the photographs of him, and although it's set at its usual jaunty angle, his face does not match the jauntiness.

'Right!' Hiroko hisses at us and we stand up and unfurl our banners. We stand there silently, the banners making the only noise as they snap in the breeze. Most of the audience doesn't even notice us, and I think only Oppenheimer and the college principal can really see what the banners say. The sun is fierce now and Oppenheimer shields his face from it, as the college principal gives a speech, droning on about how we have all been saved from tyranny.

When Oppenheimer starts to talk, his sunglasses reflect the sun directly at us so that all I can see are twin images of the sun, dazzling circles of light on the dark plastic, 'As I stand before you I feel very privileged and honoured. Honoured to be invited here today, and privileged to be alive. Privileged to be American. Which is, of course, a simple accident of birth. My family was German, and if we'd stayed there instead of coming to America, would you now think me a hero? If I'd built the bomb for the Germans, as Heisenberg tried to do, would you be honouring me? But I would have only been doing my job. Like I did for the USA.'

The audience is silent. Very silent.

'We live in the afterglow of the Bomb now. Nothing can ever take it away. But I ask you all, each and every one of you, to do what you can to ensure that it is never used again. Thank you.'

As he sits down again, the students' placards and banners slide onto the grass. The students look thoroughly deflated, they've been expecting a comic book monster and he's let them down by being human.

The college principal has struggled to his feet again, 'Thank you Professor Oppenheimer for that... interesting speech. Please allow me to present you with this medal.'

As Oppenheimer lets the medal be hung around his scrawny neck, Hiroko jumps up, 'Mr Oppenheimer!'

Both the college principal and Oppenheimer freeze.

'Mr Oppenheimer! Are you sorry for what you did?' She didn't tell me she was going to do this.

He seems to think about her question before he answers it, 'Sorry? No, I can't say that I am.'

And she dodges past us in our seats and runs up to the stage and lunges at him, clawing at his face so his glasses tumble off and we see his eyes for the first time. They look like burnt holes. One of the male students is right behind her and I am momentarily jealous, thinking that she has planned this with him, but then he grabs her and pins her arms back and I realise it is a boy from the bureau. One of Walter's boys.

'Sorry Professor Oppenheimer,' this boy is saying. 'Don't worry, I got her. We knew there'd be trouble.'

The audience are all turning to each other and saying *can you believe it?* and *fancy that*. But I cannot move, I'm stuck in my seat. I can't go to her because then she will know I'm one of them and that I've been lying to her. But then, she has lied to me, too. I feel heavy with the knowledge of all this lying, and I struggle to stand up.

'Ok, Stan?' the boy calls to me, 'Walter told me you were seeing this oriental piece.' Hiroko struggles against him but she is caught too firmly.

'Where are you taking her?' I ask.

'Just to the bureau. You can pick her up later, after she's cooled her heels.'

'Hiroko...' I say, not knowing what to say next, but she saves me the trouble.

'You bastard!'

So now she hates me.

For some reason Brecht did not expect the HUAC hearings to be filmed, and as he takes his seat in the witness stand he tries not to look self-consciously at the large camera whirring away in the corner. This is very good, even more people will be able to see his performance this afternoon. He smoothes down his blue boiler suit and winks at Helene, sitting in the public gallery. He has not worn this old worker's boiler suit for several years and it is a bit tight around his middle. There is too much food in America.

The congressmen are all smoking so he lights up a cigar. It will be a good stage prop.

The main interrogator is a man called Stripling, 'You were a member of the Communist Party in Germany, Mr Brecht?'

'No, I was not.'

'Have you ever made an application to *join* the Communist Party?'

'No, no, no, no, no, never. I was an independent writer. I think it was best for me not to join any party whatever,' and he puffs some smoke towards the camera.

'Mr Brecht, since you have been in the United States, have you attended any Communist Party meetings?'

'No, I don't think so.'

'You don't think so?'

'No.'

'Well, aren't you certain?' Stripling looks exasperated.

'No – I am certain, yes.' There is some quiet laughter from the public gallery and he smiles at them.

'You are certain you have never been to Communist Party meetings?'

'Yes, I think so. I do not think so. I do not think that I attended political meetings.' He is taking care to speak very slowly and with a much stronger German accent than usual.

'No, never mind the *political* meetings, but have you attended any *Communist* meetings in the United States?'

'I do not think so, no.'

'You are certain?'

'I think I am certain.' This is easier than he thought it would be. These people are idiots, why should anyone be afraid of them?

'You *think* you are certain?' The laughter is louder this time, and Stripling glares at the public gallery before continuing, 'I would like to ask Mr Brecht whether or not he wrote a poem – a song, rather – entitled, "Forward, We've Not Forgotten."

'*Forward, we've not forgotten our strength in the fights we've won.*

Forward. March on to the power, through the city, the land the world;

Forward. Advance the hour. Just whose city is the city? Just whose world is the world?

Forward, we've not forgotten our union in hunger and pain, no matter what may threaten, forward, we've not forgotten

We have a world to gain. We shall free the world of shadow; every shop and every room, every road and every meadow, All the world will be our own.'

Did you write that, Mr. Brecht?' He is clearly embarrassed at having to read poetry aloud.

'No. I wrote a German poem, but that is very different from this.' The laughter is quite loud now, and Stripling sits down abruptly.

The Chairman turns to the man on his left-hand side and says, 'He is doing all right. He is doing much better than many other witnesses you have brought here.' He then says in a much louder and slower voice, as if Brecht is a halfwit, 'Thank you very much, Mr Brecht. You are a good example.'

I go over to the bureau to get Hiroko. They let me into the little dusty office where she's being kept, an office I know is used solely for such purposes, having used it myself a few times. I figure if I don't go and get her out, she won't ever speak to me again. She probably won't anyway. But I need to try.

She's sitting on the desk, her arms wrapped around herself. She looks cold, even though the day is still hot, 'You asshole! You were a spook all that time? You were just using me to check up on Mr Brecht!'

'That's not true. Anyway I don't think you ever believed my journalist cover, did you?'

She's silent so I carry on, 'You were suspicious anyway. But you went along with it.'

'Because I liked you! You were gentle.'

'Because you figured you could use *me*!' I've had a few hours to think about this, and it seems as true as any other reason.

'How dare you turn this around! *You're* the one who's a fully paid up stooge for the Government! You should be apologising to me!'

'It's my job, Hiroko. It's only listening. Nothing more. It pays for gardenias and hot chocolate,' and I try to smile but she is still furious.

'You don't know, do you. You're so naïve. You think you give this information to your Government and it just reads it and files it away. What you do affects people! Look at Mr Brecht, having to give evidence to that stupid committee on his beliefs!'

Aside from all the anger there is something odd about what she has just said, 'What do you mean, *my* Government? It's yours too.'

'No it's not. *My* Government wouldn't spy on people. *My* Government wouldn't pick American people who had Japanese parents and lock them away for years on end and forget about them. *My* Government wouldn't put children into camps. My Government would act fairly for all people, regardless of their colour or race. So, no, it's not *my* Government.'

'It was a war. Lots of terrible things happened,' I try not to think about some of those things, the bodies of my fellow soldiers twisting in the sea off Okinawa.

'They didn't have to do it. It didn't help the war, did it? Locking up thousands of civilians. There wasn't any evidence whatsoever that any of them were in touch with the Japanese Government.'

I could say many things now but I know I have lost, so I remain silent.

'You don't know, Stan, do you? What it's like to be locked up for years and years. That dreadful burning sun, rising over the flat brown earth day after day. There was no shade out there in the desert. Nothing to do except walk from one end of the huts to the other, and back. We used to play in the dirt, draw patterns in it. Sometimes we'd have lessons in one of the huts, the parents would take it in turns to teach us. Someone would tell us about American history, the civil war, the constitution, and I'd stare out at the endless land and wonder why we were there.'

I wonder who she's talking to. It certainly isn't me.

'Once, I remember looking out of the window and I thought I could see two suns. Of course, it was just a reflection in the glass. But it seemed to me that nothing was normal in a place where there could be two suns.

'Even after I was let out of the camp with the other kids to go to college, it didn't end. Those days in August '45 when the Bombs were dropped, the people around me were nervous, afraid of my reaction. But you could tell they were excited by it as well. That was the disgusting part. They were excited by the – extremeness of it. It was like they'd been mesmerised by the blasts.

'Why did they drop two bombs, and not just one? It's like a murderer shooting his dead victim over and over again, peppering the body with bullets. It was unjust.'

The room feels very empty and silent, and I have to wait a moment before daring to speak, 'Did I mean anything to you?'

Her head snaps back so that she can glare at me, 'You have no right to ask me that. No right at all.'

Back in the café where it all began. And Walter is there with me.

'We need to talk, Stan.'

'What about?' I am weary, I haven't been sleeping so well.

'Your little friend. You didn't tell me about everything she had planned for that demonstration.'

'I didn't know.'

'Well then, she didn't tell *you*,' he pauses so I can remind myself just how little Hiroko did tell me. 'You see Stan, none of this set-up worked very well. We let you carry on seeing her because we figured it would be useful. But – you got too involved, didn't you? You didn't really want to screw information out of her, because you were too busy trying to screw *her*.'

I can't be bothered to say anything to him. I think about turning round to look at the waitress's legs but it seems like too much effort.

Perhaps Walter realises just how tired I am and how sad, because he changes the subject, with obvious tact, 'The hearings are going pretty well. All your information was very useful.'

'Really? Seems Brecht made a laughing stock out of us.'

'Oh no, he did very well indeed.'

'But I heard it on the news reports. He was mocking it all. The way he spoke…'

'Doesn't matter how he *sounded*. If you look at the transcript it reads as though he showed up, and he answered the questions. Means the other guys have to do the same now. And *that* means we've got plenty more work on the go, Stan. No one's going to have to take any trains home to Chicago.'

'Milwaukee. I'm from Milwaukee.' I catch sight of the waitress's legs. Shapely, definitely shapely. But still they don't cheer me up.

'Whatever. Anyway. We've got another nice little job for you. You know that guy Oppenheimer? He's got a file as long as your arm, but there are a few loose ends. Ideal for you. And we won't need you to translate any German poetry this time!'

Back in my room, I chew a lukewarm frankfurter. I could move from this place now, I'm earning enough for a better room, maybe even one with a kitchenette. But this place kind of suits me. I can imagine the waitress here. She wouldn't need to take off her grubby apron, I wouldn't mind.

I should be out there, working, gathering information. But after I'd had to translate some of Brecht's poetry for the hearing I'd got into the habit of reading it. I pick up my notebook and thumb through it until I reach the poem that keeps singing in my head:

Just whose city is the city?
Just whose world is the world?

The search for dark matter

I used to fly apart all the time. There was nothing at my centre and everything around me was so attractive that I could not stay still and quiet. I was always moving around from the last place to the next. It was exhausting but I could not stop.

I remember once getting on a train, running down the platform and clambering through the last open door just as the whistle was being blown. I didn't know or care where it was going, I just needed to feel that jolt of acceleration pushing against my bones. And when we arrived and the train seized to a halt inches from the buffers, I just waited a little bit before it turned around and I came home again.

But 'home' didn't really exist for me. I had a house with stairs I could run up and down. A garden full of trees that waved their branches at the sky. And a husband. At first he knew how to anchor me with his kisses, but that didn't work for long and I started running. On Sunday mornings I would fling back the blankets and leap out, before he could come at me with the cups of tea and try to drag me over to his half of the bed.

At night, the sky was either bright with the Moon the colour of my wedding dress and more moth-eaten each month, or dark with cloud and unmet desires. At night, I pushed him out so I could escape the wrestling, his knees and elbows always in the wrong places. I gave him a telescope and sent him out to measure the sky and count it all up. He had a double entry book where I taught him to write down the stars.

I was exhausted but still I had to move. By day I worked in a laboratory where they weighed the air. A large column of it pushed down on my scales, and I had to make the needle point upwards by balancing the air with iron weights. Some days were light and other days heavy and it took all my skill to keep the system steady.

At home my husband was full of holes, gaps so many and so various that I could not stop moving in and out of them. I searched and searched for something to stop me flying away from him into the sky.

I made mistakes. The error bars were so large that anyone would have fitted. The first one was a short man who squatted over me. His feet planted on the hotel bed either side of me and his soft penis curled on my stomach kept me there, but only for one night before I was on the move again.

I learnt it's best if you can't see them. In the dark you can make them large enough to fit your need. The next one was a man in a club. I never heard him speak because the music was too loud, but the air escaping from his mouth tickled my ear and made me laugh. He trapped me against the wall outside the nightclub and I liked the feeling of his skin on my stomach. But outside it was too quiet, and I could hear him lessen the size of himself as he talked his way into my pocket. As soon as he finished I floated away again, leaving him tiny by the side of the road.

I calibrated my need until I understood what I was looking for. There's the right person for everyone, you just have to keep hunting.

I finally found him at the end of the garden, by the fenced-off wasteland where the foxes fought. I couldn't see this man and we never spoke. His hands curved around mine and the rotten wood gave way beneath us. The fit of him was so marvellous I knew he was the one, and this was the way it was going to be from now on.

Daytimes in the lab became boring. The air always stayed the same weight, the same column of nothing drifted far above me. I got so good at it that the error vanished.

I could only meet the man on nights dark enough to hide

in. He kept his distance during the daytime, but that was alright because then he couldn't shrink into the sky like a used balloon. And if I didn't know who he was, I could keep playing the game without having to win every time.

Each morning I would see Mr X at the bus stop. He was the same height as the man and his fingers looked the correct size. He smiled at me but never spoke.

Each evening I would see Mr Y tidying his garden, his wife helping him to select the weeds. I thought I could smell foxes on him but maybe it was her. He smiled at me but never spoke.

Mr X stood next to me on the bus, stroking words in a book. Mr Y's wife waited in front of me at the butcher's and asked for her meat to be minced. Mr X walked ahead of me in the rain, water caressing his hair. Mr Y stacked flowerpots by his front door in neat piles, but one day they were broken. Kicked over by foxes, so his wife told me.

One night the man wasn't there. I waited for him until dawn, when I could see how near the foxes were, all sitting in a circle around me. They had been watching me during the night, that was for sure.

I cried and couldn't go to work. The column of air toppled over and suffocated everyone and it was my fault. All I did was sit on the sofa and feel the emptiness in my arms and legs. I didn't even know his name. I thought I was bigger than him, so how could he leave me? My husband didn't mind. He brought me cups of tea on trays and showed me his favourite stars in his book. He had caught all the double stars; the bright stars and their dim companions.

The men in the daytime were still there, and they still smiled at me but I didn't smile back. He could have been either of them. Or both, perhaps they took it in turns. I should have bitten him on his face, the way that foxes do, and looked for wounds in the daylight. You can't hide everything.

My husband ran out of stars to catalogue and he started on the spaces in between. He said it would take a long time because there were so many of them and they kept growing. He said it would keep him busy at nights and I should not wait up for him.

So I lay in bed curled up under the sheets. When I went to the window I could see the black shape of my husband as he worked on his catalogue. All night I watched him grow larger and after he came to bed in the morning, he was so heavy that he was able to push the night back into me and we went hunting for new spaces together.

Furthest south

The countdown to the Antarctic winter has started this week. If Joe looks out of the window from his work pod in the base, he can see the deep twilit sky, as the Sun hovers just below the horizon. Day after day. What would only take an hour or so at home is stretched out here into slow motion. In a few weeks it will be winter, and they'll all be living in pitch-black.

The final lot of overwintering scientists are due to arrive on the plane tomorrow and after that they're physically cut off for seven months, until October. Living in the space station must be similar to this.

The entire base is sitting on top of a giant experiment buried in the ice, which is designed to detect sub-atomic particles called neutrinos. These particles aren't rare, in fact they're very common, but they're difficult to detect because they hardly interact with anything. They whizz straight through people, through the Earth and out the other side. The ice is needed to screen out all other interference so the experiment can pick up the interactions when they do occasionally take place. The neutrino detectors are little glass balls suspended on strings of wire and buried two kilometres down below the surface. Joe and the others sit in their base, an aluminium capsule on top of the ice, watching the results of the detections which appear as flashes on their computer screens. It's his job to maintain the detectors, check the wiring, and make sure everything stays connected even during the worst of the winter weather.

This experiment can't be done anywhere else in the world, there's too much interference from daily life, from mobile phones and TV and cars and planes, and from the sheer mass of other people. So Joe took a break from the lab and came out here the year before last. Now he's back again for another long Antarctic winter.

After a meal of soya burgers he goes to his room and tries to fall asleep. He quite often suffers from insomnia here because there are no natural cues for sleep, so he's had to invent his own; a train of soothing thoughts, images, ideas. Sometimes it works.

He imagines the glass balls suspended in ice deep below as he lies in his bed with the down quilt pulled up to his chin, although he knows he will get too hot later and have to throw it off. Now, the neutrinos are in his head shedding white cotton-wool trails, like the ones that planes leave behind them in the sky. The neutrino trails criss-cross the blue sky. But blue is problematic.

Because she's also in his head, wearing her sky blue dress, the one she wore that summer. He remembers slipping the thin straps of that dress off her shoulders and feeling it fall to the floor beneath the two of them. Because of the hovering Sun, the immobility of day and night, he feels jammed up against all his history. Here, she left him only a few hours ago.

And in that same time frame it was just a hundred days ago that the explorers died. Scott and his men were the first people to reach this place, to struggle up the mountainous glacier and clamber across the surface of the sastrugi frozen into ridges and furrows by the constant wind, to see the crystals form in midair and make rainbows.

There is a peculiarly lifeless quality to the air here on the polar plateau that Scott remarked on in his diary and Joe has felt it too. This is not the sort of air that helps you breathe, it stops you in your tracks and makes you gasp. This air has the coldness of death in it. The giant black cross which is the memorial to Scott's expedition stands only a few miles away from the base, and all over the continent there are natural features named after those men: mountains, glaciers, bays.

Unusually, he sleeps well for eight hours, then he gets up for his work shift. The plane is due to arrive at midday, and he's looking forward to it, it's the last new thing before the winter. After that everything will be routine, and utterly predictable. He knows that if he tries, he can find a comfort in that routine.

The detectors are all working fine, their outputs are flashing on his screen so he goes to the kitchen to prepare a snack. Outside the plane touches down on the ice, and he watches through the window as everyone scrambles down the metal steps. A small huddle of people in Gore-Tex and goggles, one man is taller than the rest. They disappear round the side of the base and then he can hear them as they enter the boot room, laughing and talking. He could go and welcome them, but the soup's nearly ready, and they'll all be spending plenty of time in each other's company soon enough.

So he gets a shock when the kitchen door opens and Smith walks in. Joe should have known that he was the tall one. Larger than Joe, larger than everyone else. He grins at Joe and sits down opposite. Joe doesn't stop eating, he doesn't even look at him. He stares down into the soup bowl. Red tomato soup.

'Hey, how's it going?' Smith asks.

Joe doesn't reply, he just finishes his soup and washes out his bowl, before drying it and putting it away in the cupboard. It's important to be clean and tidy here, otherwise people start arguing and everything falls apart. Seven months with Smith. He didn't expect that.

Almost ninety percent of the instrument is submerged in the ice below them, very little is visible on the surface, which is just as well because it has to be protected from the weather. But each afternoon Joe needs to go outside and check the wiring. Today is no different, in spite of Smith, so he goes to the boot room and prepares himself. Two layers of outer clothing, a balaclava and goggles. And boots of course.

Outside, every tiny feature of the landscape casts long blue shadows. His own body stretches out huge towards the horizon. In this environment it's difficult to know what the true size of things is, because there's no way of comparing what you see in front of you with what you already know, and your eyes play tricks on you. He watches the pilot climb back into the plane. There's just one short moment when he wishes that he was on the plane too, but what would he be going back to? Then he checks the wiring. And then it's back inside the base.

He does the same walk around the detectors each day and it feels pathetically utilitarian compared to what Scott and his men coped with. A round trip of a few metres to check the wiring and he's feeling almost comfortable in the cold weather because he's wearing so many insulating layers.

Just one of the many reasons for Scott's expedition was to collect emperor penguin eggs, and the trip to the penguin colony had to be carried in complete darkness at midwinter before the eggs hatched. Some of the men from the expedition trekked hundreds of miles to reach the penguins, with nothing but a canvas tent to protect them when they slept. At one point during a particularly vicious blizzard the tent blew right off, and all they could do was lie in their sleeping bags buried in snow and sing hymns to keep their spirits up.

The first evening with all the overwinterers is always an occasion. The eating table is set quite formally with napkins and wine glasses, and they toast each other. Joe makes sure he's sitting at the other end of the table from Smith, but even so, he can't help noticing him. Although he's never been here before, Smith looks quite at ease. He's the sort of person who fits in anywhere, he picks up the routines, the customs. They all laugh as he describes how he was sick on the plane journey, and someone gave him a hanky so he could mop his face. Joe thinks he wouldn't have given him a hanky.

He can't get to sleep that night, perhaps he's eaten too much, or something else has unsettled him. He runs through the images but he's finding it difficult to imagine a sky blue dress when the sky here is now flushed deep red. And when he does get to sleep, finally, there's no comfort to be found in his dreams. Just a lot of bodies and it's difficult to tell if they're asleep or dead. In any case they don't respond to his touch, and he wakes, sweating.

The base is divided into three sections: work, play and sleep. There's a communal living room and kitchen and everyone has their private areas. They're encouraged to personalise them, to decorate them with photos of loved ones from home. That is what it says in the welcome manual. This is supposed to keep them calm and happy, and make them feel that the base is home for as long as they're here. Of course, it doesn't help to realise that the base itself is sinking. No base lasts here for more than a few years before it gets buried by the snow and ice. They are surrounded by the submerged remains of at least three or four older ones. The last one is occasionally seen in good weather, the edge of its corrugated metal roof an inch or two below the surface, casting a grey sheen to the snow.

Today, when Joe checks the detectors, he notices that some of the wires have worked their way loose even though there hasn't been much wind yet this winter. He mends them and goes back inside to check the detections. They're fine, perhaps a little fainter than usual, but nothing to worry about.

He likes watching the light flash on his screen. It's a random process, but on average you get about one flash every five minutes. Neutrinos are so ghost-like. They fill the Universe, they travel through bodies and minds without anyone ever being aware of them. He likes the idea that there's something happening deep below that gets transmitted to the surface where it becomes visible to him.

At lunchtime, Smith appears as Joe's eating his sandwich. He hangs around, putting Joe off his food so he gives up and pushes away his plate.

'You finished with that?' Smith points at it.

Joe nods and turns away so he doesn't have to watch Smith eat the remains of the sandwich in his wolfish manner. He has a big appetite. He looks like a bigger version of Joe, he takes up more room and makes more noise. That may be the reason for what happened, or it may not, Joe supposes he'll never know for sure. She didn't explain it to him and at the time, he didn't want her to. Now, sitting here, he'd like to know. You need to know everything you can in life because there are too many unknowns.

'Thanks,' Smith says, 'for your leftovers.'

Joe can't resist that, of course, 'They're not always leftovers, are they?'

'Pardon?' He's wiping his mouth on his fingers and he looks up.

'What you take from me isn't always left over. Sometimes I haven't finished.'

But Smith doesn't respond to this, making Joe feel a bit childish and obvious in his animosity; he just belches loudly and walks away, so that Joe is left staring at the crumbs scattered on the white surface of the table. Honestly, you'd think that whoever designed this place would have had the sense to include some colour. Outside is just endless white, so inside they could do with a little variation. Joe refuses to wipe away Smith's crumbs, even though they're supposed to keep everything clean and shipshape. But this isn't a ship.

That afternoon Joe just sits and watches the flashes. He doesn't feel like doing any work.

Neutrinos are almost but not quite nothing. They're fragments required by some cosmic accountant to ensure that energy is conserved in certain sub-atomic interactions. They're colourless, flavourless, textureless. They fill our skulls, stream through our bodies, wash past our fingers and toes. And after working on them for so long Joe feels suffused with them, as if they've thickened his mind.

After the days in the lab spent watching weightless flashes of light manufactured in wires, it was a relief to get home and hold onto her. Understand the way the freckles were distributed on her back, listen to how she'd mispronounce his name, 'Yo'. That was the way they would say it in her country, she told him.

When you meet someone, you realise there aren't just new ways of describing the same essential aspects of them, they bring to life new categories that you'd never dreamt of. Before he met her he hadn't realised how interesting he could find the nape of a girl's neck, or the insides of her wrists, or the hollow beneath her ankle bone. She gave Joe this knowledge. He was never sure what he gave her in return.

She even had an interesting job. She was the public engagement officer for the physics department, she went round schools and encouraged kids to be planets dancing around the sun in the playground, or electrons dancing round an atomic nucleus. She said there was always a lot of dancing. It was challenging to get the kids interested in neutrinos, but she tried, she said.

In return, he told her about the neutrinos. But he realised how difficult it was to describe them. You need them in physics, they're essential, but they don't seem to have any properties. They are themselves and that's about it. But he tried to dress them up, make them interesting, give them attributes, names even, but now he realises it wasn't enough. And towards the end, when he opened his mouth to speak, he'd feel the neutrinos lying on his tongue. His words were blurred by them. He became nothing but mass. He had no spark, no soul, no attributes. The ghost in her bed.

So he would sweep her hair off her shoulders and show her her own reflection in the mirror, but he couldn't make her understand how lovely she was to him. Perhaps she didn't care that he found her lovely.

And now Joe isn't surprised that she turned from him to Smith. He has a permanent image of them in his head, Smith on top of her and his back all covered in sweat. And the sky blue dress crumpled on the floor next to the bed.

It's dark now, properly dark all the time. Smith seems to be everywhere in the base. He's large and loud, and even when Joe can't see him he can still hear his voice. So one day, Joe takes a break from work and decides to do something different. He'll visit the memorial. He didn't do this the last time he was here, that whole winter the memorial felt out of reach, a bit like a lighthouse marking the edge of their known territory. It was something he'd always meant to visit but never got around to. Well, now he's going there, if nothing else but to avoid Smith for a few hours.

He looks at the map before he leaves, just to make sure he knows where he's going. The snowmobiles have got GPS on them and once the destination is loaded into them it's pretty much point and shoot, but he wants to do it the old fashioned way, by studying a piece of paper and working out the bearing. It seems fitting. That's the way the explorers would have done it.

Of course, it's further away than it looks and the wind is cold, even with two balaclavas and thick goggles. But it's exhilarating and Joe realises this is the most he's travelled in over six weeks, the furthest he's been from other people. Out here is properly dangerous. If the snowmobile broke down and a blizzard started, he would be buried in snow in minutes. And the others wouldn't risk their lives to save him. That's the first thing you learn here, don't risk your own life. Otherwise they'll all go down.

The memorial looks smaller as he gets nearer. This is a well-known optical illusion here. There is nothing else to compare the size of the cross to, so your eyes get confused and think that it's large, then it's small. He doesn't get right up close to it, he stops the sledge a respectful distance away and stands there facing it. He wants to feel an emotion, but all he can think of is Smith.

In his worst sleepless moments, he thinks Smith's done it on purpose and come here just to torment him. Taking her wasn't enough and now he's got her, he's come here to gloat about it. He hasn't mentioned it but then he doesn't have to. Just his physical presence, the bulk of him is a constant reminder of what happened.

Joe makes an effort to think about the emperor penguin eggs – the men pulling the sledges through the dark for weeks to get to the colony, eating pemmican and cocoa each evening, telling each other tales as the snow and wind battered their tent. When one of the men finally returned to Britain and visited the Natural History Museum in London to deliver the eggs to the scientists there, they weren't even interested. Things had moved on in science, they said. The eggs weren't needed anymore. The men had been in the Antarctic for too long. They'd lost touch.

Wherever you are on the base your eye is always drawn to the cross. There's nothing else to look at. Something in those men's minds as well as their bodies got them to the Pole. Something indeterminate, weighing less than the swish of air across the sastrugi and not trapped beneath the ice. The cross is only a metaphor for it.

He's sitting back in his work pod later than evening when Smith appears. The flashes are even fainter, even though the wiring looks sound, and Joe's not sure what the problem is. Smith fills the doorway of the pod. For the first time Joe wonders what he's actually doing here and why he's left her behind for so many months.

'One of the detectors has broken,' Smith says.

Joe continues looking at the screen, 'I don't think so,' he

says, 'I checked them all this morning.'

'Well, it's broken. Kaput.' And Smith makes a slicing motion with his right hand. 'You want to go check it?'

'That is my job,' Joe says with obvious sarcasm.

'Great. I'll come with you,' and he smiles. Joe can't avoid noticing how guileless his smile is, as if he's genuinely enjoying this encounter.

'I can do it by myself.'

'Sure, but it'll be an adventure for me.'

'You're easily pleased.'

In the boot room it takes him forever to get ready.

'Want a hand?' Joe offers as Smith tries to cram his feet into endless layers of socks. But Smith just keeps grinning, 'Wow, this is so exciting!'

That's when Joe realises, she left him for Smith because Smith's happier. He's just more fun to be with. There wasn't anything special about Joe apart from the neutrinos, and they weren't really his anyway.

Outside, the wind is starting to pick up and Joe knows they shouldn't be out here too long. He uses the torchlight to guide them both over to the ground array of detectors. Sure enough one of them is flapping loose wires out of the back, like spilled black guts. It'll be a major job to repair this, so he tells Smith that they need to go back inside for now and plan the work. As they turn to leave he flashes his torch into the distance, in the direction of the memorial. There's no way the torchlight is powerful enough to illuminate the cross so it's a futile gesture, but not everything that they do here has to be useful.

Inside, Smith shakes his head free from the balaclava and goggles.

'You need to hang everything up,' and Joe points to his snowsuit left lying on the floor, 'keep the place tidy, otherwise it'll turn into chaos.'

'Sure. Sorry,' and he obediently bends down.

Later, Joe's in his pod, drinking his evening hot chocolate

when Smith appears yet again.

'Smith,' Joe says, wondering what his first name is. What she called him.

'Still at work?'

'I like watching the neutrinos flashing,' he sips from his mug. 'I find it soothing.' Then he regrets saying this, he doesn't want Smith to know anything about him. He wants to be a smooth, opaque surface.

'You do know you're not actually seeing the neutrinos themselves, right?'

'Yes of course I know that.' He knows the neutrinos are invisible and what they actually detect is the light from the interaction between the neutrinos and atoms in the ice. For some reason Joe wishes he hasn't been reminded of this.

'I prefer the light in the fridge.'

'Ha ha,' but Joe refuses to smile at him.

'You know –' he is leaning against the doorway now in a chummy sort of way, as if he's been here all his life, and Joe has a sudden horror that the rest of the winter will be like this, Smith telling him things that he doesn't want to hear. He wonders what it would take to engineer a way out of here. If you get ill, really seriously ill, wouldn't they have to come and rescue you?

'You know – I think I'm really going to enjoy my time here.' And he smiles at Joe again.

Another detector breaks and this time they plan a trip outside, a longer trip to do some fixing. It's tricky because you have to be able to use small screwdrivers while wearing mittens, so some manual dexterity is called for. He tells Smith what to do. At first Smith drops the screws in the snow but he gets the hang of it all surprisingly quickly. Quicker than Joe did in his first winter.

'What's that?' Smith asks. The Moon is full and the cross can be seen way off, marking the edge of their known space here.

'It's a memorial. To Scott and his men.'

Back inside they both pad to the kitchen to get a snack. Joe can tell that Smith's finding it hard to stick to regular mealtimes in the never-ending dark.

Smith opens a tin of soup, pours it into a plastic bowl and places the bowl into the microwave. The two of them watch the bowl revolve as if on a circular stage.

'When I was a kid I tried to stick my hand in the microwave while it was on.'

'Sorry?' Joe doesn't understand.

'I used to imagine what it would feel like to be zapped by invisible rays. Microwave man!' Smith is grinning but he also looks a bit embarrassed. 'Guess I read too many comics.'

'I put some ants in a microwave once,' Joe has just remembered this. One boring summer holiday and an ant infestation in the kitchen driving his mother mad. He lured them in with a sprinkle of sugar.

'And?'

'They survived. They just kept running around. They must have been too small to get zapped.'

The ants searched out the edge of the glass tray, exploring their new surroundings while he watched. He doesn't remember rescuing them afterwards, they must have climbed through the vents and got lost in the invisible workings of the microwave. Now he wonders if they ever made it out again and back to the sugar.

Later that night Joe takes the printout of the next week's work shifts to Smith's pod to show him his allotted tasks. Smith turns his computer screen away from Joe, but not quickly enough and he gets a glimpse of sky blue. So, her image is down here in the base with the two of them. And for the first time Joe wonders what she's doing, now that she's by herself at home for all these months. Has she found yet another man to stroke her arms and talk to her about invisible, imaginary particles swarming through us all? Smith must be wondering. He can't be certain of her. There must be some doubt in his mind, given her history.

Joe talks Smith through the work shifts but he's not sure he's listening. Perhaps they should sing hymns to each other while the storm howls overhead.

A week later and they've reached the other side of midwinter. From now on they can look forward to the light. They have a dinner to celebrate and send emails to the other people overwintering on other parts of the continent. Nobody else has to undergo as much darkness, because none of the other bases are as near to the Pole.

After the dinner, Smith comes up to Joe and says, 'Have you ever been to that memorial?'

Joe nods. 'Why?'

'Quite fancy going to have a look myself. Want to tag along?'

Joe surprises himself by saying yes. 'But,' he adds, 'I think we should do it the old-fashioned way, the way they would have done it. Just walking. No motor sledges.'

Smith looks a bit taken aback, 'You're kidding, right?'

'No,' Joe knows he's got him now.

'But it's miles away.'

'Do you know how far those men walked? Hundreds and hundreds of miles. And we'll have GPS bleepers on us. They'll be able to find us and dig us out if anything happens.' Sometimes futile and maybe heroic gestures are what's needed.

'That's a relief,' but Smith still looks worried.

They arrange to do it the next day. There hasn't been any new snow for a few weeks, so the surface underfoot is hard and relatively easy to walk on. The main problem is coping with the sastrugi. Smith isn't used to this, and he soon starts to lag behind Joe. Even through his balaclava and helmet he can hear

Smith's feet slap against the frozen ground, and every now and again he slithers down the crest of a sastrugi in a way that reminds Joe of cows skittering down the ramps of lorries when they arrive at abattoirs.

The grave is two miles away and they can't walk faster than a mile an hour. A round trip of four hours. They have food, chocolate and nuts, in various pockets. Nuts don't really freeze so they're ideal.

Joe realises he's coping with Smith being here. He's helpful around the base, even if he is messy, and he's always cheerful. That counts for quite a lot, here.

And he never actually found them together. There was nothing that obvious to make him realise what was going on. But he could picture it, and now the picture's become a reality in his head. Whatever happened between them was undetectable, undefinable, but Joe could tell. It was the way they seemed aware of each other, even when they were at opposite ends of the room. Joe knew that when she ran her fingers down his chest, it was Smith she was thinking of. When Joe talked about their work, she imagined Smith describing the same work. Even the very words Joe used seemed to be contaminated with their affair. There's no such thing as purity, except maybe in neutrinos and ice. And dead men.

It's hellishly cold. Joe doesn't think he's ever been out so long in winter here and even with all these layers on, his fingers are beginning to go numb. They're wearing head torches but the narrow beam of light is no match for the Antarctic winter and for the first time he realises just how alone the two of them are. Two tiny specks of warm flesh on that vast frozen plateau.

Finally they reach the memorial. Smith looks done in, so Joe digs a chocolate bar out of his pocket and hands it to him. He gives Joe a thumbs up.

Joe's never been this close to the memorial and without the motor sledge it feels eerie. He bows his head and stands there, trying to think about the expedition that brought these men here. But Smith, recovered now with the help of the chocolate, has bounded away across the ice to read the inscription on the cross. When he walks back, he asks Joe, 'Is this actually their grave?'

'No.' His mouth can only shape a handful of words, 'There isn't a grave.' He'll have to leave the rest of the explanation for when they've returned to the base and are defrosting with the aid of hot soup. The bodies are deep in the ice now, several metres under the surface. And because of the movement of the glacier and the ice over the past hundred years, the bodies have travelled some distance. Nobody knows where they are, so they're everywhere on the plateau, spread out under the ice and all mixed up with the detectors. The men are as ghostly as the neutrinos, and as present.

The wind is picking up so they turn and head back to the base. Smith's in front of Joe now and he obviously thinks he's mastered the art of the sastrugi. He hasn't yet learnt that some of them are hollow and can't bear your weight. There's no way of telling before you step on one, but perhaps Smith's right. You may as well plough on, not knowing.

The need for better regulation of outer space

The GPS was the first clue – for us at least – that something had gone wrong. Day after day on the school run it insisted we were somewhere else. Snarled up in traffic in Saigon, stuck outside a checkpoint in East Jerusalem, or battling our way through the waves to St Kilda. We took the GPS back to the shop, but they said there was a problem with all the satellites now and they suggested we buy an A to Z.

That was the same day we tried to watch the cup match on Sky, but the pitch was covered in echoes of past games all piled up on each other like pages torn out of an old book. Electric ghosts of players scored goals against themselves over and over again, at least until the TV burst into flames. It just couldn't cope with all that information.

Then the satellites started crashing into each other like celestial dodgems and all the astronauts in the space stations were trapped, waiting for help that could never reach them. It got to the point where we could go and sit outside at night, reading our books by the light of the debris catching fire as it slammed around above our heads.

Some of this debris was large enough to survive the atmosphere and reach us on the patio, and we wondered why it had been so important to launch a coffee cup or a retractable pencil into outer space in the first place, and whether the astronauts had been slightly too ambitious in their choice of poetry anthologies. And exactly how much the dead millionaire had paid to have his ashes launched into space, complete with a brass plaque engraved '*for all eternity*'.

We could use the coffee cups, but the poetry was a bit

charred around the edges and frankly second rate stuff, so it went to Oxfam. The ashes sat on the mantelpiece and glowed as if they were being resurrected in heaven. That was ok, but the body of an astronaut still strapped to its ejector seat was too much. It only just missed our greenhouse and made a crater in the lawn.

Now there's no more night and the sky's turned into grey junk, so we're having our summer holiday in the living room. We're pretending it's Glastonbury under the dining table, converted into a shelter in case any more debris rains down.

Identity theft

In 1935 an official removed my grandfather's citizenship, ignoring the scars inflicted at the Somme, and the medal awarded to him for bravery (he'd only been following orders, after all).

On the wall of the official's office was a diagram that reminded my grandfather of biology lessons at school. Green peas can be bred from yellow ones, but he couldn't remember why this was so. How can greenness (or was it yellowness) lurk invisibly in a generation of peas before reappearing in their offspring? Now, as the official ran his finger up and down the lines connecting black and white circles, my grandfather wished he'd paid more attention at school.

Then, after passing through the deaf and blind city streets, the official let himself into my grandfather's apartment. It was his duty to confiscate my grandfather's complete set of Beethoven symphonies, for safekeeping. The official scratched his Mendelssohn records and scribbled on the pages of his Kafka.

But my grandfather could keep the theory of relativity, Communism, and that nonsense about the unconscious. So he set off for England, with Freud, Marx and Einstein to keep him company on the boat.

Long before Crick and Watson discovered the double helix structure of DNA, my grandfather could have told you about the twin strands of German and Hebrew knotted around his tongue. It was a difficult job to unpick all this and splice English words into it – words he accumulated from reading Dickens, jam jars, Orwell, army orders, ration books, newspapers, advertising hoardings, railway tickets, Joyce, laundry labels, street signs...

I never met him, but I inherited from him a dislike of Wagner, and a predisposition to diabetes. His collected works of Dickens, with German words pencilled in the margins, are all mixed up with my books on my shelves. I trace the marks he made; hoping his interpretations can be trusted when I'm on holiday in Munich, swigging back the beer at Oktoberfest.

And so it goes on. When I say 'Aye' in my South London accent, a Scottish friend laughs at me. It's not my word, and anyway – why do I want it? But I'll pick my way through your language. And like a magpie stealing shiny buttons, I'll take what I want for my stories.

The equation for an apple

Robert stands outside the physics department and watches his supervisor's office through the window. He's been standing there for some time now, maybe half an hour or more. Other students have passed by, and asked him what he's doing, but he hasn't replied. Everything in the office is grey or black or white, the dust-covered desk, the blackboard with its mathematical hieroglyphics, the sun-bleached curtains bunched up on either side of the window. The only thing with any colour is the apple. He chose it especially for its redness and beauty, and he's left it on the precise centre of the desk.

He's waiting. He's waiting for the door to open and Blackett to enter, sit down at his desk, notice the apple, pick it up and take a bite from it.

He has never seen a dead person. That part has only happened in fairy tales, not in a cold physics department in an English university thousands of miles from his home. Perhaps it's all make-believe, it certainly doesn't feel real to him. Nothing does, not anymore.

Robert has only been in Cambridge for a few months. He was an outstanding student in Harvard and he expects to be equally fêted in Cambridge. His tutor in America recommended that he should work with Rutherford, the genius who cracked the secret of atomic structure. But Robert has never done any lab work before, and Cambridge is suspicious of this boy who claims to be able to understand relativity but who doesn't seem to know how to carry out simple measurements.

So in his first week there he is given some test tubes to wash. The sink is at the back of the students' lab, which is in the basement of the physics department. He is not used to washing things. Other people have usually done this for him in the past.

He can't figure out how to remove the chalky residue from the bottom of the test tubes. He tries scraping it out with a pencil. He tries dislodging it by spraying water into the test tubes – with disastrous results. He stacks the still dirty test tubes in an inexact pyramid on the draining board from which they roll onto the floor and smash, one by one. He watches them all smash without attempting to stop them, before he fetches a dustpan and brush.

All the walls in this lab are tiled, like in a hospital, or an asylum. After the fragments of glass have been swept away, he runs his fingers along the regimented gaps between the tiles and waits for some truth to be revealed to him. Something better than errors and dirt.

In the second week he is given an experiment to carry out. The instructions are typed on yellowed paper lying in a folder on the wooden lab bench and at first Robert is pleased by the idea of carrying out this task, showing them what he can do. But he has always lacked interest in the physicality of Bunsen burners, wooden benches, lead blocks and microscopes. And now he needs to master them all.

The instructions tell him that he must create oil drops by spraying oil between two horizontal electrically charged metal plates. Then choose one of the drops to view through the microscope. Adjust the voltage across the plates so that the oil drop is made to hover motionless in midair by the electric field between the plates counteracting the force of gravity. Calculate the corresponding electric charge on the drop caused by the field. Repeat for different oil drops and analyse the different charges obtained, to calculate the smallest common denominator. This is the charge of an electron, that indivisible kernel at the heart of matter.

Before this, the only electrons he has known have been

symbols chalked on blackboards, components of equations represented by letters or numbers. Never real, hovering right in front of his eyes.

But he can't make it work. The oil canister leaks onto his jacket (his fine wool jacket bought in Boston to impress the English scientists), and when he finally manages to create some oil drops, they either fall too quickly or rise straight up to be caught on the plates and burnt by the high voltage. The battery leaks acid and corrodes the bench, and the lab assistant – a taciturn fellow who doesn't speak to anyone – shouts at him.

After about a week of fiddling with the battery, he stumbles on the right voltage needed to make the drops hover, but he can't focus the microscope because his fingers are covered in oil, so that when he looks through it all he sees is a miasmic blur of yellow, like looking at the sun with your eyes shut.

The lab soon smells of frying oil, and the diagram detailing the layout of the equipment in the instructions bears no resemblance to the mess he has created. He lays his head on the bench, and hides his face in his arms to avoid looking at it all.

Back at his lodgings there is a letter from his mother. She has written that she and his father hope that everything is going well with his studies as they haven't heard from him yet – *'but maybe you are too busy to write. I picture you in a punt, wearing a straw hat, reading poetry with the other students. There must be so many picnics on the river and May Balls!'*

He is assigned Blackett as his supervisor, but Blackett is not much older than him. And worse, he fought in the war, spending years in the trenches.

'He had a good war,' another student says – mystifyingly – to Robert who is asked to see Blackett in his office, to explain how he is getting on with the experiment.

A very tall man, with his back turned to Robert, is looking

out of the window. It is bright outside, one of the few sunny days since he arrived here. He would like to be out there rather than having to explain himself, and account for his lack of progress.

Blackett does not turn round immediately so Robert has time to scrutinise the back of his jacket, its ordered pattern of checks with lines crossing under and over each other. What will he say? How can he explain?

'Ah, Oppenheimer, my dear chap,' now Blackett is facing him, smiling. Robert is confused. He holds out his hand, ready for this miniature battle of strength. But instead Blackett turns back to the window, as if the view outside is more interesting than his new student, 'How are you finding things here?'

'Very well, sir!' Robert can't resist the temptation to sound enthusiastic.

'Good, good… And where have you come from, precisely?'

'New York City.' Or is Blackett referring to his university? 'Harvard. I'm a Harvard man.'

'Good, good. You did study physics there?'

'Yes sir. Of course.' What does Blackett think he's doing here if he hasn't studied physics before?

'But you haven't done much experimental work, I gather,' and now Blackett turns round again and winks at him. He doesn't know what to say to this. Is he a joke already? But before he can think of a reply, Blackett has moved on. 'And your digs? Are they satisfactory?'

'My –' what did the man say?

'Lodgings.' His manner doesn't change. He must be the same with all the students who think they are clever enough to come here, and who fail at the first hurdle.

'Oh they're excellent, sir!' He tries not to think of the inadequate bed linen and the breakfasts of pale undercooked eggs.

'Please, we don't stand on ceremony here. Just call me Dr Blackett,' and he smiles again to show that their talk is finished.

He is surprised to be invited to the pub with the other students. So far they have been a homogeneous mass, and he has found it impossible to differentiate between them. There are about five post-graduates altogether, and two of them are apparently Rutherford's students. They refer to him as 'the old man.'

'The old man wants you,' one of them will holler across the lab, and the other one will sigh theatrically.

In the pub he sips his first pint of English beer, trying not to wince at its tepidness. Perhaps in a cold climate like this they find lukewarm beer a comfort. He wonders what they drink in summer, what he himself will drink then, but he can't imagine being here in warm weather, wearing his shirtsleeves rolled up, having finished the wretched experiment and started on his real work.

One of the students is telling the others a story. This student, Robert thinks his name is Lubbock, is also one of Blackett's and has nearly finished his PhD. It seems to be a funny story, because they're all snorting and guffawing into their beer.

'What do you think of that, Oppenheimer?' Lubbock grins at him.

'What?' he hasn't really been listening, he can't follow their accents very well.

'Oppenheimer,' one of them jolts him out of his thoughts, 'where are you from?'

'New York City. And Harvard university,' he says automatically.

'But where is your family from – originally?'

'Originally? Why – New York.'

'Oppenheimer,' the student says again, more to himself than Robert, drawing out the individual syllables as if testing them against some idea in his head.

'We're an established family, we've been settled a long time in the USA,' he tries to smile and jiggles his feet, uncomfortable in their stiff new brogues. It's not particularly true, Robert and his younger brother Frank are the first generation to be born in America, but there's no question about their patriotism. He's managed to convince his landlady to call him 'Robert' mainly to avoid any discussion of his family name.

'So, what's the answer to the experiment?' he asks, keen to change the subject. They must have been through the same ordeal as he is now facing. Surely they broke the test tubes, and smeared oil on their clothes. But now they look at him blankly.

'That's not the point,' one of them says. 'The point is the doing of it. We could tell you the answer but you'd still have to do the experiment.'

He knows the answer anyway, he went to the library to look up Millikan's original paper. He just wants to know if they will help him, but it seems they won't.

'How long have you spent on it?' Lubbock asks him.

He tells them, and one of them whistles in amazement, 'That long?' He nods.

They don't ask him any more questions after that. They start to talk amongst themselves and after a bit he gives up even pretending to be part of them, and he fishes out a small book of modern poetry from his jacket pocket.

The next day Lubbock comes into the lab and walks over to where Robert is trying to adjust the microscope. 'There's a trick to it,' he says without any preamble, 'there always is with these things. You have to show it who's in control. Just like with women.'

'I don't need any help,' says Robert, feeling resentful.

'There,' Lubbock ignores what he has just said, 'that should work for you now.'

And it does. It is a miracle. When Robert looks through the eyepiece (having first cleaned his glasses) he sees a single, perfect oil drop shining in the afternoon sun. He turns to thank Lubbock, but the lab is empty again.

'I've never seen such large error bars,' laughs Blackett in his office the next day. 'They stretch the entire height of your graph!'

'I still managed to get the right answer,' Robert says, feeling his face flush.

'Oh, you went to look up the original paper? Probably just as well. You could have derived any answer you like from this,' and Blackett waves his hand at Robert's lab book, dismissing it from further consideration.

Robert's known as 'the poet' by the other students but he can't tell if this is affectionate or not. He goes to the pub with them and once he's figured out the custom of buying rounds, he makes sure he buys more rounds than is required, so they continue to invite him along. Even though most of the time he sits there reading while they talk around him.

Occasionally, he joins in when their talk strays into more theoretical subjects. He can't resist showing them what he knows. He is desperate to be known for something. So one evening, when they start to talk about relativity, he has to interrupt.

'No,' he says, 'you've got that wrong. Time actually does slow down as you approach the speed of light.' And he jots down a few equations on the back cover of his poetry book.

One of them says, 'Perhaps we should just stick to the maths and avoid any sort of description with words. Perhaps we don't have the right words.'

Robert nods his head, 'When I want words, I read poetry.'

They don't know how to respond to that so he's left alone again as they talk amongst themselves about sport, rugby perhaps. He's a little unsure about all these English sports which seem so important to everyone here. Blackett rides, he knows that. That's the only outdoor pastime which appeals to him, he spent last summer staying in a ranch in New Mexico and each morning he'd ride high into the mountains. Once, during an unexpected rain storm, he got off his horse and sat underneath it for shelter, watching the steam rise off its flanks. In the afternoons the women in charge of the ranch would welcome him back and fetch him platters of sweet fruit: grapes and oranges.

'There was a girl, once –' he starts, thinking of a friend at school, but she wasn't pretty enough for this recollection, and was also too friendly and too keen, so he elides her with another face that he can only just remember. A woman at the ranch. Black hair, swift graceful movements. He never dared speak to her.

They glance at each other, 'You've got a girl?' they ask him.

He nods, 'She's beautiful. Smooth hair, eyes the colour of cornflowers...' but he can't think of anything else to say about this half-imaginary composite woman. He stops, and takes a gulp of beer.

'Sounds better than the ones at Girton!'

He nods again, grateful for their assumption that he is telling the truth.

'Have you seen them?' Lubbock says, 'all bespectacled and respectable,' he laughs. 'Covered in flannel from head to toe, and not allowed out without chaperones. In case they get impregnated by us in the lecture theatre or in the middle of the street!'

Robert coughs to hide his embarrassment. But they are science students, they should be able to talk about the facts of life. 'Are there any women here?' he dares to ask, hoping to sound like a man who is at ease around women. The beer is slipping down quite nicely now. He could get used to it, he supposes.

'Only wives,' someone sighs, 'and wives are no good. Although they will talk to you. But generally they resemble middle-aged horses. Particularly Rutherford's.'

The others nod, 'You'll see them at the departmental party next week. You're coming to that?'

He is. The fat white envelope with the invitation to this annual party is almost the only correspondence he has received from anyone in England since he moved here.

'Some of the wives are better than others.'

'You're talking about Mrs Blackett? She's a peach!'

Robert has the chance to verify this for himself because when he arrives at the party Mrs Blackett is standing in the shade of a low, wide apple tree, wearing a dress of some soft fabric. Blackett's next to her, so Robert is able to go over and be introduced before Blackett spots Rutherford and wanders off.

Robert panics about what to say. She shuts her eyes, in fact her whole face seems closed, she doesn't seem interested in him so he allows himself to stare at her.

Dark hair, carefully curled and lying close and neat against her head. Long eyelashes. A small mouth. He settles on the mouth, realising now that he hasn't looked at any women at all, apart from his landlady, since he arrived. Cambridge is a male city. Male students, male lecturers, male servants. His landlady is a great doughy loaf of a woman, with two small currants for eyes. She looks like she should be a capable housekeeper, but she's not.

Finally Mrs Blackett opens her eyes and looks straight at him. Her eyes are, as he predicted in the pub, cornflower blue. He is not used to his predictions being accurate. He stares back at her. He's aware, horribly aware, of his messy hair that resists all brushing and sticks straight off the top of his head as if he's been electrocuted. Right now, he feels as if he has indeed been jolted by electricity, some sort of shock is leaping through his body, making him feel more alive.

'What did you say your name was?' She speaks so softly that he has to move closer to her than seems entirely respectable.

'Oppenheimer. Robert Oppenheimer.' He clears his throat and waits.

'How exotic,' and she smiles at him, 'how exciting to have such a – different name. So much more interesting than Jones, or Smith or even Blackett...' Her voice is low with a faint tremor to it, reminding him of the one and only experiment he has ever managed in the lab, making a dynamo spin round in an ever-changing electromagnetic field. The thrilling hum of this motor vibrated through the bench and seemed to kickstart something deep inside him. Is her tremor due to nerves? Robert is not used to imagining the thoughts or feelings of other people. Besides, she has just called him exotic. He knows he doesn't fit in here, but until now he has felt that this is his own fault, that he lacks something. He hasn't realised until now that it is because he is simply different, and that this difference might even be interesting to someone.

She's close enough to touch. Off to one side, about fifteen yards away, he can see Blackett and Rutherford, hear their loud, cheerful voices. The old man is talking to Blackett at the same time as trying to light his pipe and Robert can hear him cough and can smell the sweet, rich tobacco. The sun is caught by the leaves on the tree above them, and he watches as Blackett's wife is covered in moving shadows. Perhaps everything will turn out alright in this place, after all.

'Do you know whose tree this is?' she smiles at him. Her teeth are as white as china cups.

'No, whose? Please do tell me,' he tries to smile back.

'Newton's. It's where the apple fell on his head and he had his brainwave.'

'Gosh.' And he is genuinely impressed. This is where it all started, the great synthesis of ideas and observations that makes their subject. The realisation that what happens out there in the sky, what moves the planets around the Sun is due to the same force that makes the apples fall from the tree. He is standing on the very spot that Newton once stood on, and maybe he too will have an amazing idea and change the world.

'Is it really that extraordinary? Patrick told me all about it, but I'm not sure I truly understood.' She frowns a little, as if slightly cross, 'I must confess I don't usually understand what he says to me, when he talks about his work.'

And now Robert can picture their marriage, Blackett's

endless tiresome chatter about physics and departmental business colliding with her unspoken wish to be left in peace, to eat breakfast in silence, to be adored without words. Robert would adore her, if she would let him.

She runs a hand over the smooth mass of her hair, 'Why don't you try and explain it to me? Perhaps they have different ways of explaining things where you come from. I might understand it better.'

The apples on the tree are still small at this time of year, not much more than promises of fruit. He talks to her about Newton's theory of gravitation, about how everything in the Universe is governed by this same mysterious law, and she smiles every so often, and once she lays a hand on his arm.

'We're eating from the tree of knowledge,' she says. Her breath is scented with the weak sparkling wine they have both been drinking, 'You and me and this tree. All we need is the serpent.'

He feels bold enough to say, 'If this is before the Fall, then we should be naked and innocent.'

She laughs, 'Oh, it's too late for that, Mr Oppenheimer. Far too late for innocence. For me, anyway. Maybe you can still be saved from whatever delicious sin you're tempted to commit.'

He is trying to tell her about Einstein, when Blackett wanders over, 'Time to go, dear.' As she allows herself to be led away by her husband, she nods at Robert with a little dip of her head.

'See you in the lab, Oppenheimer!' Blackett booms at him.

Robert is finally given a proper task to do. According to Blackett, this will be a nice job, something to get his teeth into. He hasn't seen Mrs Blackett since the party, over a month ago. He knows that Blackett sometimes invites his students over for Sunday lunch, but he hasn't received an invitation yet. Perhaps it was wrong to use that word – *naked*. Or perhaps she has simply forgotten about him.

He starts his task, working away in his office, far away from the lab and all its mess and dirt. He needs only pencil and paper, and his own thoughts. Blackett has set him a deadline for this task, he must deliver a seminar on it to the other students in a month.

He feels like a character in a fairy story or a Greek myth, having to overcome challenges before he is able to win the heart of the beautiful princess. He tries not to think of Mrs Blackett, silent and invisible behind grey stone walls. He picks up his pencil and starts to work.

Finally he receives an invitation to lunch. Lubbock is invited too.

'Damned nuisance,' Lubbock says, 'I really need to spend every minute on my thesis.' But he doesn't look too upset.

'What's the form?' Robert asks.

'The form?' Lubbock sounds puzzled and Robert worries if he's used the wrong word. But he has to get things right. 'Oh, just wear your everyday clothes, nothing fancy. It's all very relaxed in their house.'

This worries Robert. He can cope with formality, with clear rules. It's the unspoken customs that trip him up.

The Blacketts live a few miles outside the city in a small village and on the day of the lunch Robert decides to ride over there. He hires a horse, and the feeling of the animal moving beneath him reminds him of the freedom he felt in New Mexico. But this countryside is not the same. It is so flat that he is surrounded by sky, and he feels like he's in an upturned bowl or lab dish, being inspected by some celestial experimenter.

By the time he arrives at the Blackett's he is sweaty and it seems to have been the wrong thing to do, although nobody says anything. All of them, the Blacketts, Lubbock and even the Blackett's maid, look surprised to see the horse. He has been long enough in England to know that surprise is designed to indicate bad manners on behalf of the person doing the surprising. There is the language of words which he initially thought he spoke in common with the English, and then there is the language of gesture and habit which he knows he doesn't understand at all.

As he stands in the Blacketts' garden holding the reins of the horse which is showing far too much interest in the apple tree, Mrs Blackett directs the maid to fetch blankets and towels and pails of water without ever once looking at him. Lubbock and Blackett stand some distance away talking physics. He is hot. He thought England was supposed to be cold, but it is damned hot. Only the people are cold. He removes his jacket and drapes it over the horse which is now cropping fallen apples as they lie in the grass. He wipes his forehead and resolves to say something brilliant to Mrs Blackett.

He gestures at the apples, 'The fruit of knowledge.'

Mrs Blackett replies, 'Do come inside for lunch, it'll get cold. Come on Patrick, come on Mr Lubbock.' She still hasn't looked at him. Perhaps she's wearing the same dress, he wishes he could remember the pattern of the earlier one. It may be a sign.

Now he has no choice but to troop into the dining room. From there they can all look out of the window and watch the horse as it starts to eat the remaining apples on the tree.

'Won't it get colic if it eats too many?' asks Lubbock.

The maid serves them soup, and they are silent as they spoon it up. Robert finds he is aching from the ride, he must be out of practice.

'So,' Blackett starts, 'electrons.'

'Patrick,' Mrs Blackett murmurs, 'it's Sunday. No talk of work, please.'

As he sips his soup which has a peculiar jelly-like consistency, the only sound is the clatter of cutlery. Blackett and Lubbock both seem content to stay silent if they're forbidden to talk about work. But he has better manners than that.

'I remember what you told me,' he has managed to get

through the soup and gratefully abandons the spoon, 'that afternoon.' He dares to look at her but she is still gazing at the horse, 'About the tree. Newton's tree. Remarkable to think it's survived all this time.'

She gestures to the maid to clear away the bowls, 'Newton's tree?'

Robert stares at the wrinkles in the tablecloth left by his soup bowl. Is she going to pretend she didn't tell him? That they didn't talk together, didn't exchange the words *innocent* and *naked* with each other?

Blackett looks over from the top of the table where he is attacking the meat with a carving knife. 'Newton's tree?' he repeats, and he chuckles, 'that's the story we like to tell visitors to the University.' He lays on a plate the thinnest, greyest slice of beef Robert has ever seen. 'But Newton wasn't even in Cambridge when he came up with the idea of gravity. He'd gone back to his family home in Grantham, because of the plague.'

The plate is handed across the table to Robert. They all watch him as he is invited by the maid to help himself to roast potatoes and boiled vegetables. The vegetables slither off the serving spoon in a sort of greenish mass. He is not sure how many roast potatoes he should have and they are all watching him, so he serves himself just one. Perhaps it will compensate for the horse eating all their apples.

Mrs Blackett glances at her husband, 'Patrick dear,' she murmurs in a way that seems designed to sound private, 'do make sure our guest gets enough to eat. In America they must eat so much more meat than we do here.' Another thin grey slice of beef lands on his plate.

After lunch the horse is clearly paying the price for the apples and won't let itself be mounted, so Robert has to lead it all the way back to the stables, six hot and aching miles away.

His mother has written to him, '– *and, my dearest, by chance I met Mrs Powell who suggests that you do write to her daughter. They all know you meant no offence by your remarks. But if I may offer some advice about women –*'

Robert screws up the letter and throws it onto the floor. On his journey to England he hoped to leave Mrs Powell and her daughter behind, ideally somewhere in the mid-Atlantic to be eaten by fish. But he cannot pick and choose what to remember and forget, because to his horror even Harvard itself is now wavering in his mind, the brick sidewalks lead to impossible destinations, the seminars have faded to murmurs and even his own prized essays are just tangles of words. He looks out of the window at dull sky and stones and tries to superimpose on it a picture of New York City, its streets so alive with all hope. It can't be done. That image feels like heaven, something once believed in that has fallen away. Cambridge is reality and everything else has dwindled to this. He presses the nib of his fountain pen into his thumb, hoping for the skin to break, for blood to appear, for some sort of transformation. But the clock ticks on and he is left with schoolboyish ink on his fingers. Maybe it would be easier if he had a knife.

He should reply to his mother. He packs the pen away in the desk and makes prints on his blank writing paper with his inky thumb. Finger prints are unique, so perhaps these blots say more about his character than mere words could do.

The following week Lubbock gives a seminar. He's due to report on the work he's done for his PhD. Robert is keen to see what Lubbock is capable of, so he gets to the lecture theatre early and takes a seat in the front row. As the others arrive he realises he is sitting amongst the faculty, the lecturers and professors. Rutherford is two seats away, next to Thomson, and Blackett is at the end of the row. Between them are some other men that Robert hasn't seen before, perhaps they're visitors to the department. Twisting his head, Robert can see the other students are all at the back. There is a collection of empty seats between him and the rest of the students. He wonders why they don't sit closer to the faculty.

Lubbock enters, picks up a piece of chalk, turns his back to the assembled staff and students and starts to talk. As he talks he writes strings of equations on the board.

The lecturers on either side of Robert fall asleep, their heads resting on their chests. The one to the left of him makes a slow mooing sound, the one to the right of him snorts in sharp bursts. Blackett is awake, and clearly following Lubbock's work.

Robert can't understand what Lubbock is saying because the words are muffled and disappear into the black surface of the board, but he can understand the equations. It is standard stuff to do with a basic application of Bohr's model of the atom. He has done all this stuff before, at Harvard. He relaxes, he is still ahead of the others.

Lubbock has made a mistake. Robert glances at Blackett who appears not to have noticed so he gets to his feet and points at the offending equation, 'Say, that bit's wrong.'

Lubbock falls quiet. Robert goes up to the blackboard, and takes the chalk from his sweaty hand. He wipes part of the board clean and chalks up the correct version of the equation, 'There you go, it should be easy from now on,' before going back to his seat.

The rest of the room is silent, Lubbock included.

In the pub later, he stands at the bar, watching the beer splash into the glass. He is buying Lubbock a pint, by now he knows what he likes to drink. And Lubbock looks like he could do with a drink. After Robert's intervention he didn't really seem to get back into his seminar, he carried on making mistakes and couldn't answer the questions at the end. Robert had to answer one of them for him.

Robert carries the pints over to the table where the students are all sitting. Sometimes the lecturers join them for this post-seminar drink, but not today. Nobody looks at him as he rests the heavy glasses on the table.

'Say,' starts Robert, jiggling his foot, 'all that twiddling around with Bohr's model. It's a bit old hat.'

Lubbock slowly raises his head from his pint, 'Old hat?' he repeats.

'Yes,' says Robert. They're not normally so quiet. He thought they were beginning to warm to him, but now it feels the way it did at the start of the term, when he was in the lab breaking things.

Blackett appears, and the students sit up a bit straighter. He doesn't normally come to the pub. 'Oppenheimer, a word please?' he murmurs, so Robert has no choice but to get up and follow him outside.

Blackett stares at a point on the wall of the pub some distance from Robert, before speaking, 'It's not usually the done thing to interrupt a man when he's giving a seminar.'

'But he'd made a mistake! I was just helping him!' Robert tries to stop his voice from squeaking.

'It was his talk. His responsibility to explain his work to the audience. Not yours.' Blackett smiles now, and remains standing there, feet planted wide apart on the pavement. Robert sees now why he was a loved and admired officer in the war. 'Here,' and Blackett holds out a ten shilling note, 'buy Lubbock a drink. I think he's earned it. And yourself of course.'

Robert can picture Blackett handing out largesse to his servants and although he wants to fling it onto the ground, he has to pocket the money. And Blackett isn't quite finished with him, 'We must go riding together sometime. I'd enjoy that.'

He can't go back inside the pub to face Lubbock. All he can do is trail back to his lodgings and work out how it has got to this. When he arrives there, he finds another letter from his mother, '*Dearest, we didn't quite know what to make of the fingerprints and the blank sheets of paper in your last communication to us. Was this a sort of English joke? Or perhaps you simply forgot to include the actual letter! Anyway you will be pleased to know that we have managed to book passages on the Queen Mary – at very short notice – so that we can visit you.'*

He checks the date of the letter, they will be in Cambridge a week from now. He hides the letter in his desk, along with Blackett's money.

The day before they arrive he goes to the market and uses Blackett's money to buy a bag of apples.

'Keep the change,' he says to the astonished greengrocer.

He wants to give Blackett an even chance so he takes care to dip only half the apple in the liquid. The tell-tale smell of almonds is so strong he's afraid to even breathe it. Perhaps it will fade away once the liquid dries.

He waits until lunchtime when he knows Blackett is dining at his college, before he goes into Blackett's office and sets the apple on the desk. For a moment he thinks about eating the apple himself, before he leaves the room and goes to wait outside.

The nearest help is a million lightyears away

Not long after we started seeing each other, we lay in the park one spring afternoon and he picked a flower out of the grass. I hoped he would tuck it behind my ear, but he just pulled the white petals away from their yellow centre until the flower fell to pieces.

Then he unlaced my shoes and rolled my tights down.

'Not here, not in daytime,' I said, 'everyone can see us.'

But we can't meet at night because he has to work. He works at the observatory and he's bought me a laptop with a webcam on it, so he can watch me lying in bed when he's operating the telescope.

'I want to call you Daisy,' he whispered in my ear. He never uses my real name, he doesn't like it.

It's his job to monitor the planets around dying stars and observe them as they fade into endless night. He once told me, 'Soon we'll have telescopes sensitive enough to pick up distress signals from the planets. But we still won't be able to reach them in time. All we can do is watch.'

He touched me between my toes and then between my legs, he's always very methodical about things like that. I felt so sorry for him as he arranged me on the sun-warmed grass, he must have seen more life coming to an end than any other human being. That's why I make allowances.

That sinking feeling

Einstein's in a lift. The front of this lift is a concertina mesh of metal, so he can peer out at the illuminated floors of the building as they float up past him.

He lives in an apartment at the top of this building with his wife Mileva and their two boys. He is a professor at the University where he is highly regarded by his colleagues for having published a series of papers which revolutionised physics. He should be working on the next paper now but instead he is going to visit his lover. He feels no guilt at this visit, the ragged remnants of his home life no longer justify that degree of emotion.

Earlier this morning at home, the boys were fighting over their rocking horse and Einstein watched as Mileva tried to separate them and stop them knocking into the furniture. The small room was jam-packed with overstuffed armchairs, a bookcase holding stacks of papers as yellowed as stained teeth, a dresser displaying a not quite entire set of china decorated with mechanically identical pink rosebuds. The silver cutlery was hidden away, but the presence of the knives gave a sullen metallic edge to the room.

When they first got married and were given so many presents, he and Mileva had laughed at them all. They told each other that they were not going to let themselves be crushed under the carved wooden sofas and crystal decanters and glass ornaments and brass pokers and lace antimacassars. They could continue to live as free spirits, working together on their studies. But they had had to move into a larger apartment because the old one wasn't large enough. Then the children had come along and it turned out they needed even more belongings and now whenever Einstein thinks of his wife, he pictures her hidden underneath the mound of bottles, quilts, diapers and wooden toys that seems to accompany her wherever she goes.

The lift moves slowly as it clanks its way to the bottom of the building, and Einstein is getting impatient. But he tries not to show this because he is not alone. A little man in a fancy uniform operates the lift; it's his job to crank the concertina shut, pull the lever up to start the lift on its journey, and crank the concertina open at the end of the journey to let the passengers leave.

A typical conversation with Mileva might start like this, 'Why don't you ever talk to me about your work anymore, Albie?'

He winces at her use of this old pet name, but she doesn't seem to notice.

'You used to show me what you were working on, so that I could help. Spot the mistakes in your workings.'

Even as he sits at his desk trying to work, she bustles around straightening out the piles of papers and blowing dust off the desk.

Mileva was the best in her class at school. She wanted to go on and be a physicist, and her family paid for her to go to college where Einstein met her. Small, dark, witty and intense, she was the only girl in their physics class.

Now and then he catches her flipping through the books in his study. It doesn't seem to matter which book, it could be about set theory, logic, mechanics or calculus. She turns the pages fast, as if she's thirsty and gulping down cold water. Sometimes he clears his throat and she puts the book down and runs out without saying anything, or she lays the book to one side and comes to peer over his shoulder at his work. He resents this, although he pretends not to. She asks questions and points out mistakes in his maths. He supposes he should be grateful, when they were students she used to check his homework and she always found all the mistakes.

When he next glances up from his books she's gone again. He goes back to the problem. *What is gravity? Why do objects accelerate at the same rate regardless of their different masses?*

As the lift continues its descent, he glances at the lift operator, at his uniform with its sad oversized epaulettes, before realising that the man is staring straight back at him. Even odder, the man is sticking his tongue out the way that kids do. He has a round face and enormous eyes, and the merest wisps of hair clinging to his pink scalp. His body seems far too big for his short stocky legs. Einstein glances at his hand, positioned on the lift lever. It is the chubby hand of a baby. And back at his face. Baby face, the tip of his small pink tongue just visible. Why has he never noticed this before now? Dear God, the lift operator is a baby.

'I do this all day,' the baby says, his hand still on the lever, 'can you imagine how I feel?'

'No,' admits Einstein.

'I don't know whether I'm coming or going, rising or falling. I never see daylight, I never see anything. Nobody talks to me apart from telling me which floors they want. They just shout numbers at me, as if I were a mathematician.'

'I like numbers,' says Einstein.

'I know you do,' says the baby, 'but do you like them more than real things? It would be nice if – just occasionally – someone thanked me. Or told me how much they admired my uniform.'

'It's a very nice uniform,' says Einstein.

'You're a terrible liar, Herr Professor Einstein,' the baby grins.

Einstein doesn't know what to say to this, he'd rather be outside where he can smoke a cigarette in peace. But this is wartime and there are no cigarettes and no peace.

They're about half way down now and the lift is picking up speed. Maybe there is something wrong with it, because it shouldn't be going so quickly at this point, but Einstein realises he is enjoying the flying sensation in his stomach, the feeling of weightlessness. He feels as if he has escaped the pull of gravity, just for an instant. He has escaped his wife.

Elsa lives in the bottom of the building, her apartment is in the basement. Here he eats cakes and drinks coffee with her in peaceful silence. Elsa's silences are almost the best thing about her, she creates a vacuum that envelops him so that Mileva's mournful questions, the boys' incessant chatter, his colleagues' boring conversations about outdated physics all fade away. She's like a cake herself, thinks Einstein, as she digs her fork into a fat puff of whipped cream; she's all pillowy and fair with strawberry-pink cheeks.

The next day as he escapes the apartment, he finds himself looking forward to riding in the lift. He is anticipating that feeling of freedom, of being temporarily cut off from the inertia of the marital bed and the gloomy clouds of his arguments with Mileva which seem to be tinted the same colour as the children's bruises.

When he gets into the lift, the baby starts to talk almost immediately, 'You're visiting your cousin because you're having an affair with her. You see her every morning for a little *schtup* and some refreshment afterwards. Sometimes you skip the *schtup* and just have the cake. That's what she prefers, and probably you do too. Neither of you are that young anymore.'

'Why –'

The baby looks at him enquiringly. The lift hasn't moved yet, the door is still open. 'Why – what?'

But Einstein can't decide what the question should be.

When he arrives at Elsa's apartment, he rushes her through to the bedroom so he can sink into her. Whenever he's surrounded by her soft body, it feels like being swaddled in a comforting eiderdown. He doesn't talk to her about his work, or Mileva, or the arguments.

And for some reason, although Elsa's apartment is the same size as his and Mileva's, it feels far more spacious. Even the heavy furniture suits her. The large woollen rugs feel soft under his feet, the chandeliers glint pretty coloured light all over the walls, the coffee cups are so thin and delicate that they are almost translucent. Perhaps she's just a better housekeeper than Mileva.

Maybe things would have been different between him and Mileva if it hadn't been for the first child. When they were still both students they went on holiday together and she got pregnant. They talked about getting married when he could afford it, but that would not be until long after the baby was due to be born. In the meantime she would go to her parents' home in Serbia to wait it out. He still has the letter from her father telling him about the birth, she had been too ill to write herself.

Lieserl. That was the child's name. She would be twelve now.

While Mileva was in Serbia he would cycle to work at the patent office, the wheels spelling out some complicated rhythm on the cobbled streets and he would try and work out how exactly his life had changed, now that he was a father. Except it all felt too theoretical, the only real noticeable change was that Mileva was no longer around so there was an absence, not an additional presence. But when she finally returned she seemed slightly shrunken, as if something had been sucked out of her.

'Have you figured out what the question is?' says the baby.

'No, not really,' says Einstein. His mouth feels dry, he needs coffee.

'Isn't it something about different masses falling at the same rate?' the baby looks rather pleased with itself, as if it's figured out something quite profound. 'Isn't it about the peculiarity of gravity?'

'How do you know all this about me?' asks Einstein.

'Because I'm your baby.'

Einstein is finding it difficult to breathe. The lift definitely feels as if it's accelerating way too fast now, perhaps it is out of control and they are plummeting to the depths of the building. They must be falling to their deaths. 'What do you mean, *my* baby?' He wipes sweat off his forehead.

'I'm your first child, the one you never saw.'

Down goes the lift, surely they must be past the basement now where Elsa is waiting patiently with hot coffee for him, but it shows no signs of stopping. Einstein can feel their descent in the pit of his stomach, and he wants to vomit.

He's sitting at his desk staring at the walls, as Mileva bangs around his study, piling books on top of other books, 'You never even saw her!' She has said this before, many times. 'You couldn't even be bothered to get on a train and visit your own daughter.'

'There was no time. I had to work and it was too far away,' he tries not to sigh because that only makes Mileva crosser, 'but I can imagine just how she looked because you described her so beautifully in your letters. Her little chin, her soft hair.'

'Those were *my* words! That's all she is to you – just words. Symbols on a page, like your work. You reduce everything to symbols; light, bodies, the Earth...'

'Don't be ridiculous. That is my job, it's what I do.' You used to do it too before you got married, he wants to add, but decides he'd better not.

'Lieserl was just a problem you had to solve, so you wrote a letter and got rid of her. That was your solution, but perhaps it was wrong.'

'You agreed!' He is exasperated now. They wrote the letter together. He signed it but she agreed to it.

'Because I had to! I couldn't just show up here with a baby!'

'You could have stayed there with her. If you'd really wanted to.'

'Don't you dare talk to me about what I wanted! You never asked what I wanted!' This comes out as a quiet scream, '*You* didn't even want to see her!'

And so they go round and round. Nothing changes, everything stays the same.

There must have been things for Lieserl, Einstein realises now. He sent money to Mileva just before the birth. Wouldn't there have been toys or perhaps a blanket embroidered with her initial in one corner, like the ones wrapped around his sons when they were both babies. He wonders what happened to all those things. When Mileva returned after the birth, she was carrying a small suitcase that seemed to weigh her down as if it were filled with rocks. Only now does he wonder what was inside.

When she is outside in the garden with the boys, Einstein walks softly to their bedroom, opens the drawer containing her clothes, and starts looking. He pushes aside piles of her underwear, pairs of the tough brown stockings she insists on wearing and corsets that would squeeze the life out of any man, until he gets to the wooden bottom. Nothing. He looks around the room for the suitcase, but when he sees something dark in the shadows under the bed he changes his mind. Let Mileva keep her secrets. He has his.

Today when Einstein leaves to visit Elsa, winter has begun and the apartment building is cold. This will be the second winter of the war and already fuel is scarce. As he gets into the lift Einstein thinks that the baby's uniform looks tattered and baggy and its eyes appear dim.

'Are you alright?' he asks.

'Thank you for asking,' the baby replies, 'your concern touches my heart.' It doesn't appear to be sarcastic.

'Why aren't you a twelve year old girl?' he dares to ask it, 'how did you get to be a lift operator?'

The baby smiles sadly, 'I could be anything, really. You don't even know if I'm dead or alive.'

Einstein stares at the scruffy braid, peeling away from the baby's uniform. It must have been a golden colour once, but now the shine has worn off and it's an indeterminate shade of brown dirt. One of the epaulettes has come loose and is flapping in the draught of air from the concertina door as the lift jerks down towards Elsa. But for the first time he doesn't feel hungry for cream cakes or sugary kisses and he wonders why he thinks he needs this plump blankness in his life.

They stop.

'You're here,' announces the baby, and cranks open the door.

Einstein stays where he is.

'Go on,' says the baby, 'she's expecting you. She bought some more cakes this morning.'

But he can't move.

'You can't be late for her. You're never late.'

When he finally leaves the lift he walks in the opposite direction to Elsa's apartment until he finds the narrow uncarpeted stairs that are only ever used for emergencies. He slowly walks up them until he gets to the street level. He needs fresh air.

In the study again, with Mileva.

'The lift operator told me that he was my baby. My first baby.'

'What! What the hell are you talking about?'

'He is a baby, actually. When you look at him properly. It makes sense.'

Mileva looks at him, her eyes round, 'Sense? You're mad.

You've gone mad.'

'Do we know what has happened to Lieserl?'

'You know perfectly well what happened. She is living near Novi Sad, with a nice family who look after her well. Just as we – *you* – arranged.'

'She's living? Really? Do we know this?'

'Well, we haven't seen her. But then you never did see her, so how would you recognise her now?'

This is so indisputably true that Einstein is silent. How would he recognise his own daughter unless someone else told him who she was? He is reliant on the word of other people. And he has learnt not to trust that in science so why should he trust that in the rest of his life? He feels dizzy, as if he's been turned upside down.

He finds an atlas and draws a line on the map from Berlin down to Novi Sad, cutting across roads, railways, mountains, rivers. Somewhere on this paper land is his daughter, but she may as well be in a different world to his. He can only imagine her as a dot in the half tones of the map, and himself on the black line of the railway track as it meanders across the two dimensional terrain, too slow or self-important or lazy ever to reach her.

The next time he sees Elsa he has to invent a reason for missing a visit. An important departmental meeting, he says, and she doesn't reply. She talks instead about trying to get her daughters married off, she thinks he is lucky to have sons. She doesn't know about Lieserl and now it feels too late to tell her.

For the first time he wonders how she manages to get hold of so many cream cakes when there is rationing. 'Can I take one home?' and he gestures at the plate spilling over with cream and jam. He has to carry the cake out of Elsa's apartment in his cupped hand, but the baby doesn't mind. Its eyes widen when it sees the cake and it crams the whole thing into its mouth.

'Thank you,' it gasps. The lift hasn't moved, the baby has been too busy eating to bother with the door or the lever.

'That's alright,' says Einstein. He pauses, 'Where do you go when you're not here?'

'Go? I don't go anywhere. I'm not real, am I? I'm in your head, man. You still don't understand do you?' Even with a light dusting of sugar on its uniform, and a faint moustache of whipped cream around its mouth, it manages to look both dignified and cross.

'But if you're not really here, then how does the lift move?'

The baby slams the door shut and starts the lift, 'Is it moving? Are you sure?'

Einstein thinks about it, 'Well, I feel the motion right here,' and he taps his stomach.

'Why does that make it real? Can you trust your memories or your feelings? You thought you were in love with your wife and here you are *schtupping* Elsa. Or perhaps she's make-believe too. Perhaps you're a junior patent officer with a girlfriend you never bothered to marry because you were both too Bohemian to do that, and a twelve year old illegitimate daughter called Lieserl who likes to go sledging in winter and owns two pairs of ballet slippers. And you daydream about beams of light and clocks and trains, and go home each evening and doodle your thoughts, never able to turn them into anything other than scribbles. And perhaps you're happy, Herr Professor Einstein. Really and truly happy. Can you imagine that?'

The lights in the lift snap off and they are in pitch-black. The lift starts to accelerate down past the basement, and as it freefalls through space Einstein finally knows what it means to be free of gravity. And all the associated grief.

No numbers

When my gran was in hospital she was so thin that her body was barely a bump under the covers. Her hands lay motionless on the sheet, her face making everything that was happening here too real for me to bear. She faced the TV although I didn't think she was actually watching it. Cartoons, football, reality talk shows; all of them edged by such definite beginnings and endings.

She was dressed in a hospital shift, her arms bared to provide access for the drips. On the first visit I took her hand and she smiled, she was still able to do that. Sitting and holding the paper-light hand of a dying woman wasn't as awful as I thought it would be, because I would have done anything to make it easier for her. Even so, my mind kept scurrying away to hide, and I had to make an effort to haul it back into this room full of machinery and pastel; lemon yellow bed sheets, peach cushions and grey oxygen pumps.

Alongside them was a more deadly colour. Dark blue ink on her left forearm creating a five digit number. Even in summer she had always worn long sleeves and one way that I knew she was ready to go was when she stopped covering it up, no longer having the energy to hide it or hate it.

This number was given to her in the camp. I don't remember when I first saw it but I always knew it was there. But it wasn't something that could ever be spoken out loud, it was unmentionable. Like the name of God.

Even when I was a kid and good at maths, I saw that there was a tyranny associated with integers in the way they marched forward with such regularity. They didn't allow for gaps. I didn't think they left any room for imagination or contradiction.

She died just as the credits rolled by for some sitcom that gets repeated regularly, something about the war that was maybe supposed to convince us that it was all over, that we were allowed to laugh about it now.

When the final measure of oxygen escaped her, I let myself stroke her arm and touch the tattoo for the first time. Ran my little finger over each of the five integers and wondered if they'd always been this blurred. There was a horrible fluidity to them, as if whoever had tattooed her had done it hastily and with no more thought than scrawling a bill on the back of an envelope.

In maths lessons at school I drew wobbly lines of Venn diagrams to solve problems. Our teacher chalked a question onto the board: *If there are twenty girls at a party and twelve have brown hair and fifteen have brown eyes, how many have both?* and I bent over my notebook, creating intersecting circles. Then she added *How many have neither?* and I realised I'd assumed they all had at least one or the other.

Now the problem was unsolvable and I crosshatched the intersection of the circles with neat red lines, covering up the mistaken numbers I'd written there earlier, thinking about innumerable crowds of blond-haired blue-eyed girls surrounding the darker girls.

'Never get a tattoo,' my grandmother said during an otherwise unremarkable shopping trip to Brent Cross, as she gripped my hand tightly. I was sixteen and just beginning to realise that she was holding onto me for her own benefit rather than for mine.

Maybe she disliked cartooned stars or butterflies that couldn't tremble in the breeze or rosebuds that would never open. Pictures that were just bad copies of real things, that provided no room for imagination. I didn't like them either, those sorts of tattoos always seemed pointless to me.

This was just a week after she'd found a packet of cigarettes in my bag and there had been a row. I was angry because she had gone through my bag after she'd smelt smoke on my school uniform. I was sixteen so it was legal, I told her. It was wrong, I was a disobedient child, she shouted, did I want to die of some horrible coughing disease? And I could tell she was thinking, I survived all that so my granddaughter could kill herself with cigarettes? I could only shake my head, and so she won.

She managed to link my disobedience to my future death in her own mind and maybe in mine too. I never smoked again and I agreed not to get a tattoo.

She was always trying to teach me to knit, helping me to bend my fingers in the correct way but everything I tried to make came out looking the same, no matter what it was supposed to be. I couldn't follow her knitting instructions, it felt like trying to crack a code. It was far more difficult than maths.

She told me stories, real and imaginary. She told me that when she came to England in 1946 she couldn't pronounce the word 'tea'. On her first night here in a boarding house somewhere near Dover she had gone hungry rather than ask someone the way to the nearest café. She had kept her mouth shut and read poetry to improve her English.

She told me that where she came from, the winters were so cold she could go skating on the lake in the south of the city, and one day the ice cracked and the water beneath swallowed up a little boy. His body was never found. Afterwards I wondered if she'd known the little boy.

She told me that her parents had owned a glove factory, and I wasn't listening properly and thought she said 'love'.

She told me she was named after the Mona Lisa because it had been stolen in 1911, although when I was older I worked out that she must have been born several years before this.

Her stories were all about the past, set in Germany and in England. But there were mistakes in them, and gaps between them. I calculated that there were about twelve years of her life which had produced no stories at all, or not ones she would tell me. But she must have had reasons for the mistakes and the gaps, and the stories all connected together in my head like her knitting stitches created around essential air. I sensed that if I asked her about the gaps then the knitting would come unravelled and the needles would clatter to the floor, where they would glint and be dangerous. So I never asked. I just listened.

At some point in my teens I worked out that I was three quarters Jewish and one quarter Irish. The Jewish part was also German, Austrian and Polish. The Irish part was possibly Catholic, possibly not. I wasn't sure which part was more important but I started wearing a Star of David around my neck. She asked me to remove it, she didn't want me to identify myself in this way. So I removed it, and I replaced it with a silver skull which she didn't like either, but which she could tolerate.

As I got older and moved onto more complicated maths I realised that there were two circles for two sets of numbers, and these numbers mapped one by one onto the people who had survived the camps and the people who had perished. No intersection between the circles, people were either alive or dead. And there was no way of knowing which particular number was in each set. Nothing to distinguish one number from another, just by looking at it.

Now that I knew so many integers had hidden histories I no longer felt comfortable doing sums with them, it felt like treading on ashes. It was a relief to learn about the irrational numbers such as pi, or e, or the square root of two. Numbers that weren't related to integers and that went on forever so I could spend my whole life following rules to work them out. It was a relief to learn about such individual and eternal numbers.

As I sat and waited in the hospital for the nurse to come,

I continued to hold the hand that was once hers. The next programme started on the TV and this one was a documentary, the screen full of light reflecting off rushing water but I couldn't work out what it was. A lake, a river, an ambitious bath?

I sat on. In spite of the pale blue curtains of the hospital cubicle flapping around me and the huff of my gran's oxygen cylinder which wouldn't stop even though she had stopped, I eventually took this in: life on Earth may have started on the coasts of lakes and seas, in places which are both wet and dry. Liminal places that are difficult to define.

I didn't ask her if it had been Walt Whitman and his declaration that he was vast and contained multitudes that she'd read as she lay on the bed in the boarding house at Dover, but it would have been appropriate, because:

She was an anti-Zionist who went to Israel for her holidays.

She read the Telegraph and voted Labour.

She ate bacon for breakfast and then cooked kosher lunches at the club for other Jewish pensioners.

She put stones on my grandfather's grave for the anniversary of his death. But she always selected three stones; one for the Father, one for the Son and one for the Holy Ghost.

She said she was disappointed in me when I explained how to jiggle coins out of public phones, yet she stole small plants from Tel-Aviv airport and smuggled them back to England in her handbag.

When I was twelve I decided to do German at school. She was upset, and then she got cross because I couldn't understand her when she spoke German to me. But her German was stuck in the 1940s, and she had to slip in English words such as *zebra crossing, package holiday, take away.* They stuck out like known desert islands frilled at the edges with guttural and incomprehensible seas of syllables.

Finally the nurse came. First she turned the TV off, then

she turned the oxygen canister off. She told me that I could let go of my gran's hand if I wanted to, that she needed to do some things. She made it clear that I should not be here when she did these things, so I went and sat on a rickety chair in the corridor. I took my gran's handbag with me; a battered old-lady's bag, the sort that was capable of holding everything from dentures to Strepsils, as well as stolen Israeli plants. I surprised myself by remembering to take her rings as well. They were in a plastic dish on top of her hospital pedestal. Two gold circles lying side by side, a symbol of two sets of numbers with no intersection. Or a symbol of infinity. I preferred infinity.

I continued to sit, although I wasn't sure why. I supposed I was waiting for the nurse to finish, although she didn't say that I should.

A hospital porter came rumbling past pushing a metal trolley. He manoeuvred it into the ward and I realised it was for my gran. He came back out of the ward without the trolley and sat next to me. I glanced sideways at him, looked at his hands resting on his lap. Big red beefy hands, a swallow drawn on each of them next to the thumbs. The two swallows faced each other with their long tails trailing across the back of each hand as if they were trapped in the process of some courtship dance. I didn't even know if swallows did courtship dances. Maybe I was imagining too much.

'Where's she off to now?' he asked, looking straight ahead at the closed doors.

'Back to the nursing home,' I said. And then Hoop Lane, I could have added. The largest crematorium in North London with vile chimneys constantly puffing smoke into the air.

'Ah.' He shuffled on the chair as if settling down and I realised he was also waiting for the nurse to finish, so he could take my gran away. He gave me a paper tissue and I realised I was crying.

I didn't like the swallows because it meant that I would

remember him, that there was something linking him to my gran. I wanted some unknowable entity – as alien as an Ancient Greek to carry my gran on a ferry off to the chimneys in the Underworld, not someone who could be classified like a butterfly with a pin piercing his hospital overalls.

'You like my swallows?' He'd noticed me looking. I didn't reply but he continued anyway, 'You want to know why I got swallows on my hands?'

I realised I was holding my breath, but I wasn't sure whether it was from the effort of trying not to cry or because I didn't want to find out about the swallows.

Just then the doors to the ward clanged open and the nurse appeared. The porter got to his feet and disappeared into the ward without looking back at me. Neither of them had said a word. I picked up my gran's handbag and I knew that I could open it now, because she was dead and she couldn't tell me not to.

The needle begins its journey into my skin. 'Won't take long,' the tattooist says and I nod, trying not to wince and thinking that maybe I should have had a farewell ceremony for my skin before it is transformed. The needle whines like a mechanical mosquito and I am bitten with ink as dark as blood. I'm anxious, wondering if it will work and if the tattoo will look the way I planned. The tattooist is confident, she keeps saying that most of the designs she does are much more complicated than mine, but I'm still nervous.

Time stretches out. The pain is insistent, keeping me in this room and stopping my mind from taking me away.

'All done,' and I lie there for a moment longer listening to the sudden silence. The tattooist drifts to the other side of the room, as discreet as a GP after some intimate examination. I wonder if I will ever get up again because I feel so heavy, as if the needle has sewn me to the chair. I try to relax my jaw, move my teeth. I glance down at the arm, it no longer seems like mine, and I wonder what it's been transformed into.

When I first thought about getting a tattoo I decided I'd quite like a picture of the bones beneath my skin, making it look like the skin had been peeled back to show what was underneath. But although I liked the idea of having a tattoo of my body, I realised I wanted something more abstract.

Finally I dare to look down at my new tattoo. The inner part of my left forearm is decorated by two thin black circles. The overlap between the circles is cross-hatched in red. There are no numbers.

I know she asked me not to do this, but I think she would have liked the idea of being commemorated by an intersection, a mathematical picture of complexities.

Safety checks

The official arrived at 9am, just as expected. I'd arrived at work an hour earlier than usual, so that I could start running the checks on the telescope and save him a bit of time. I knew he wouldn't want to miss the return bus to the city.

He was a small, neat man who looked as if he'd just been to the barber's. I'd already exchanged several phone calls with him but this was the first time we'd met face to face. His predecessor always insisted on some coffee, and so I played it safe and brewed a pot. I find it helps to pay attention to what these people might like.

The telescope was parked so that the big dish was facing directly up into the sky. Whenever I look at the smooth dish I think how amazing it is that something like this can be second-hand metal, beaten out of gunships and destroyers that have been retired from the war and replaced by newer versions. Perhaps they too will become future telescopes after they've served their country.

I was the only one to meet him at the main entrance. My staff were indoors, waiting at the controls.

The annual safety check was part of my routine. I would put the telescope through its paces, and the official would make sure that it couldn't overrun the brakes or stray into the forbidden zones around the horizon. Then he would sign off the paperwork, return to the Ministry and that would be that for another year. Once the safety check is complete we are allowed to get on with our work.

He got off the bus and patted dust from his trousers. Not all the roads up here are paved yet; apparently the Government's working on it. 'Full moon tonight,' he announced, by way of a greeting.

'It makes no difference to our work here,' I replied.

We stood outside the gate to the observatory and he looked around at the low wooden fence that enclosed the telescope and the hut. 'Not much security up here.'

'We're quite isolated.'

'I can see that. Even so, I'd better order you some barbed wire.'

He walked up the path and I followed him, he seemed to know where to go. These people always do.

'Coffee?'

He considered for a moment, 'Yes, you might bring me one,' and he opened the door to the control room. The other three members of staff were waiting in there, he nodded at them and sat down at my desk. I handed him the cup of coffee, and he set it to one side and ignored it.

I'd already logged onto the telescope control system. He glanced through the manual that I'd left out for him and started to type commands. The staff watched him closely as he worked, they're not so used to the Government as I am. They stood without speaking, as he printed off and checked the coordinates that define and limit the telescope's movements around the sky.

'Why don't you walk me through your typical set-up at the start of each evening?' he said, and he let me take my seat. While he looked out of the window and made notes, I directed the telescope to skim along inside the green line defining the edge of the permitted zone. Then, as a test, I gave it the coordinates of an object outside that zone. The blast from the siren was so loud that the staff put their hands over their ears.

At the same time as the siren started, the official reached into his jacket pocket and removed a small black electronic device. It lay in the palm of his hand as he held it out to me, indicating a small red light that was shining on and off. Then he pressed a button on the device and out of the corner of my eye I could see the telescope glide back up to the zenith, and the siren stopped its din.

'That's a new feature,' I said.

'The Minister's new too, remember? He felt things might have got a bit informal under the old administration.'

'But the telescope hasn't strayed over the green line for years.'

'Better safe than sorry,' and he put the device back into his pocket. I could imagine it by his bed at night, its red eye illuminating his dreams.

'Would you like to see our latest results?' His predecessor had seemed to show a genuine interest in our work, but this official merely glanced at the paper I'd drafted for him before he went on his way.

I accompanied him back down the path, and I noticed he took small steps the way they do down in the city where nobody has any space of their own. Up here, it's easier to move around more freely. After he'd gone I stood and waited until the sun went down behind one of the neighbouring hills and the scrubby grass lost its colour in the dusk. The birds started to roost and were as noisy as ever – we're plagued by these small brownish birds which are well so camouflaged in this environment. But we never manage to shoot any of them, however hard we try. Perhaps they've adapted their plumage to evade us over the years.

The horizon is lit up by the fires that seem to burn constantly outside the walls of distant towns. It's just luck that there's no town right here.

The observing that night went well. We're mapping the sky, to search for the dark objects. We can hunt them down by the way they disturb other objects, causing their trajectories to wobble and go off-course. It's an ambitious project, but calculations have shown that around 90% of the predicted number of these dark objects can be found in this way. That night three more objects were detected and their positions noted. I'm afraid I don't have the time to speculate as to the nature of these objects and why they are so dark, I leave that to others. After all, I have my hands full with everything else that I am responsible for.

At around midnight I turned on the radio for the news headlines. The radio has always been capricious and only works in certain locations in the control room. Each night one member of staff wanders around, holding the radio in front of them as they search for the best reception. Tonight almost everything was drowned out by static and fuzz, but we could just make out the usual daily update to the number of people arrested as a result of the disturbances. For some time, my deputy had been plotting this number on a graph on the blackboard, to see if it was changing in any systematic fashion. It looked random to me but I was never much good at mathematics. The deputy claimed to spot a long-term trend but sometimes he said the number was increasing and other times he said it was decreasing. I supposed his interest in this subject was harmless, in any case I hadn't mentioned it in my annual report.

A week later the phone rang. The official wanted to make another visit. This was most unusual. In all my time at this observatory I couldn't remember any officials coming here more than once a year. The place didn't seem to be high priority for them.

This time he accepted the coffee and drank it with quick sips like a bird from a feeder. I'd told the staff to carry on with their normal duties, this wasn't the annual check. So they were at their desks, but quieter than usual. I'd even laid out the paper about the dark objects to see if he was interested in it after all. I could have posted it to him, of course, but the post is not so reliable these days – not since the post boxes started to be firebombed on such a regular basis.

He handed me the empty cup. 'Let's get to work.' The staff kept their heads down, as if they sensed that I was being admonished by him. Perhaps I was, but I didn't remember doing anything wrong.

He motioned with his hand that I should stand up and relinquish my seat to him and then he worked at my terminal for a few minutes. I was impressed that he didn't need the manual, he must have known these commands off by heart. Or perhaps they weren't in the manual. Almost as soon as he'd stopped typing the siren started blaring, and the telescope dish started moving away from the zenith. It swung further and further down towards the ground, until it stopped, the dish hanging there in a way which had to be severely taxing the struts and supports. For the first time ever I worried about metal fatigue. But I didn't have much time to worry, because – bizarrely – even though the telescope had gone right over the green line and was now well within the forbidden zone, the siren stopped.

The dish was almost but not quite entirely facing this hut and I could stare right into it. It was like staring into an enormous eye that never blinks or sleeps. The metal completely filled my vision, and I could see the rivets that had been used to join all the different components together to make a sort of patchwork of metal plates. At the dead centre of the dish was a collection of aerials and detectors, probably like all the paraphernalia that there must be at the back of the human eye to connect it to the brain.

It was silent in the control room. I wrenched myself away from the sight of the dish and realised the official was waiting for me to turn my attention back to him.

'I have made some adjustments,' he told me, 'in the way that the telescope can be used from now on.'

'Adjustments?' As I spoke, behind me I could hear the deputy breathing, short shallow breaths.

'The forbidden zone is now the permitted zone and the

permitted zone is now the forbidden zone. Got that?' He said this quite quickly and almost casually, but I guessed that he'd practised it, perhaps in the bus on the way up here that morning.

'But –'

'What about our objects? What are we actually looking at now?' The deputy was standing up behind his desk. It was the first time any of them had ever spoken to an official.

'They were never *your* objects, were they?' he chuckled quietly, 'they are slightly too far away for any realistic claims of human ownership.'

'But –' I couldn't think of anything to say apart from repeating the deputy's question, 'what are we going to observe?'

'Just map the horizon the way you've been mapping the sky, and log everything you see. I'll come and collect all your observations on a regular basis.' He shuffled some papers together and looked at his watch, his bus was due. He started to walk out of the hut and then he stopped suddenly, 'What is that?'

The deputy's blackboard was facing him, its graph quite visible. I just hadn't thought. Before a routine visit by the official everything in the control room is checked and double-checked, but this visit caught me unawares. Fortunately there were few indications of what the graph actually showed, apart from the numbers chalked by the side of each data point. He may have recognised these numbers from his work in the Government, I couldn't guess.

'Ah – just the numbers of dark objects we have found, logged on a regular basis. It helps keep up the staff morale to show a visible tally.' I didn't look at the staff but I could hear the deputy sit down heavily at his desk and sigh, as if releasing something held inside him.

'I see.'

I followed him down the path. He was standing in front

of me peering into the distance as he murmured, 'Rub that board out, won't you, and I'll pretend I never saw it.'

I nodded, even though I was behind him and my gesture was presumably invisible to him. Then something else struck me, 'The dish will sweep right across our hut when it does its measurements. Are we to be included in the data?'

'Of course.' The bus had arrived and he climbed on board. I could just make out the back of his head as he showed his ID card to the driver. Then the bus drove off and I was left pondering my new tasks.

The story of life

The wife's bought him another shirt for Christmas. Surreptitiously he tucks it in the cupboard behind all the other shirts. A lab coat covers up everything and nice shirts are wasted when you're working with fruit flies, yeast, reagents and acids. And he knows how much she hates ironing.

On the first day back at work he gets up early, leaving the wife in bed. He pecks at the air above her face before going to make his breakfast and a sandwich for lunch, and he even remembers to wrap the last of the Christmas cake for a snack. The department's a fair distance from anywhere handy, right out of the city on the side of a glen, and there aren't any shops for miles. You have to be organised and take what you need. After ten years of working there, he's always organised. That's why he's the Gaffer, the chief technician. Other people may be the professor or senior lecturer and have their names on the website and the stationery, but he's the one who actually runs the place.

Today, as usual, he's the first to arrive. The department feels empty and disused after the winter holiday but he knows that won't last and by later on this morning it'll be full of graduate students and post-docs, all slotted into their usual places along the benches in the lab. He goes to check the flies in the fly room next to the lab, where the test tubes of fly larvae and flies are kept. On this first day back he knows the smell of the yeast will hit him like a punch from a drunk man. He also knows he'll get used to the smell and by the end of today it'll be a single hummed note as a backdrop to his work, ready to greet him tomorrow and every day after that.

The fly room is the correct temperature, the racks of test

tubes are buzzing. He doesn't look at their contents, that's not his job. He's got more than enough to do.

An email reminds him of a new post-doc requiring bench space, another one has the delivery information for the new machine arriving on Thursday.

Then it's coffee time, a pause for the cake and to catch up with colleagues, or as his assistant Lucy puts it, 'relive the pain.'

'It was venison for us this year,' he tells Lucy.

'Roadkill for your Christmas dinner? Did Mrs Gaffer hit something she shouldn't have?' Lucy always has the right response. Her work's neat too, the test tubes clean and sparkly, the reagents mixed to the right concentration, the flies dosed with carbon dioxide so that they sink as peacefully as a baby going down for its nap. So he lets her have her occasional 'Mrs Gaffer', even takes pride in this title awarded to his absent wife. Because it just reinforces what everyone knows; he is in charge.

He goes back to his desk to study the requirements for the new machine. It's a complicated piece of equipment, that's for sure. A space in the lab has been cleared since before Christmas for the machine itself, and its sidekick of a console which is needed to send instructions to it.

It'll do the boring bits of the technicians' jobs, all the piping of liquids into wells, the endless syringing that has probably cost him a chunk of the motor action in his right wrist. He's been looking forward to this machine for a long, long time.

Back home in the evening and the wife is working through a new recipe to use up Christmas leftovers. He studies the ragged meat heaped on the chopping board, 'Where *did* you get that venison from?'

She looks up from the cookbook, 'I told you.' She doesn't like to be interrupted in the kitchen, so he leaves her alone and goes to the conservatory to sit and wait for his dinner. Was it venison? How would he know? He's never tasted badger or hit-and-run dog.

It's a full moon tonight but he can't see it because the conservatory roof is – maybe fatally – dimmed with algae and moss. He should clean it. He will clean it. Maybe when spring arrives, when he can see what he's doing in the evenings.

On Thursday he gets up even earlier, keen to get to the lab and wait for the machine but something happens that morning which annoys him. There's been a light snowfall in the night and he's surprised to see footsteps already marking the path to the department. Usually he's the first.

Inside he can hear voices; the Prof and someone else – a woman? He finds them in the corridor outside the lab where the Prof appears to be in the process of handing over some keys to a tall woman who is not exactly slouching, but leaning against the wall. He's aware of her looking at him as he approaches. Her eyes are so dark there's no difference between the pupils and the irises. Her hair matches her eyes and as if in deliberate contrast, her shirt's as white as a just-laundered lab coat.

'Ah,' says the Prof, and to the Gaffer's mind he looks guilty, as if he's been caught doing something he shouldn't have. 'Good. Glad you're here. This is –' but the Prof mumbles and he doesn't catch her name. She definitely isn't a post-doc, it's not that she's too old for that, just different. As if she's taken a meandering path through life to get to this point. He knows about that sort of path, he's taken a slightly unusual one himself, and somewhat more unusual than the official version on his CV. But he still doesn't understand what the woman is doing here. And the Prof's dropped an entire set of lab keys in her hand and scurried off before anyone can properly explain to him.

'You'll be wanting bench space?' he tries. He's obscurely annoyed, he can always provide space but he needs to know in advance. These things can't be presumed. He shouldn't be taken for granted.

She shakes her head. Maybe she's a theorist visiting from

another institute, and that's why she isn't going to work in the lab. Theorists can be a bit peculiar. But if that's the case, why did the Prof give her the keys to everything?

'Office space then? In the computing section?'

She shakes her head again and he can tell somehow that she's wanting to smile.

'Forgive me Miss—' he pauses to allow her to insert her name, but she stays silent so he has to continue this rather pompous sentence, 'forgive me for asking, but what is it actually that you'll be doing here? What do you need?'

After she studies him for a moment she finally replies. 'I don't need anything. I'm a writer; I'm the writer in residence.'

He's still feeling out of sorts even as he stands with the others around the machine, fingering his plastic cup of plonk. Although the Prof did apologise after the encounter this morning. 'Sorry about that, clean forgot about her until she showed up. She shouldn't be any trouble, she's had all the health and safety training.'

'What is she actually going to do here?' But the Prof wandered off again, and then he'd been busy sorting out the ceremony.

They don't actually smash a bottle on the side of the machine, it's far too expensive and important for that. All during the Prof's speech about how it's going to revolutionise their work and bring in some much-needed money, the Gaffer is aware of the writer. When he turns to look, she's leaning against the back wall staring into her wine. For almost the first time in his life, he wonders what a woman is thinking.

The next morning and the snow has deepened. After he's crunched his way into the building, he reaches the fly room. As he's about to unlock the door he glances down and notices something small on the floor at his feet. Small and oddly shaped, and looking rather out of place in the man-made corridor.

He looks closer. It's a dead mouse, lying on one side, claws outstretched as if still trying to grasp something. Its fur is pointlessly smooth. He looks into one eye but there's nothing to see so he fetches a dustpan and brush and sweeps it into the bin. Then he washes his hands, even though he hasn't touched the body, and starts work.

Inside the fly room, he wonders. They've never had mice here before. Perhaps it was attracted by the yeast? There must be more, you never get a single mouse.

Sure enough, the next morning he finds another body. And another the morning after. Nobody else ever finds any, and he begins to feel as if the mice are dying just for him. And he always finds them in the same place, by the door of the fly room. Are they trying to get in or out?

After the fifth mouse, he tells the wife. They're eating something bird-like for dinner and he's finding the remnant bones rather disturbing. He tries to explain to her.

'Something sweet,' she says. 'That's what they like nowadays. You need a trap with a bit of chocolate in it.' She begins dishing out the pudding but he shakes his head.

He starts to measure the week in mice. One, two, three, four, five dead bodies. If there are any live ones in the building they're ignoring his offerings of chopped up Mars bars spiked onto traps. He's secretly relieved, he's not sure he wants to deal with bloody corpses. The mice show no signs of violence, and there's no indication of the cause of death.

The writer appears at his desk one morning, 'Can I see the fly room?' This is the first time she's asked him for anything so, surprised, he says yes.

She follows him into the room and he realises what a cramped space it is for two adults. He watches her peer at the ranks of test tubes on the shelves. The ones on the left hand side of the room are still larvae, not yet hatched out. It takes about twenty-eight days or so for the flies to hatch. The tubes on the right hand side are full of silently buzzing flies. He knows without looking at them the way they swarm around in the tubes, crawling under and over each other, burrowing into the plug of yeasty beige goo that's both their nursery and their food.

'You can't really see them properly until you get them under the microscope, but the flies on each of these shelves have a different phenotype.'

'A what?'

'A different physical form.' Her hair is densely black and not at all shiny, so that when he looks at it, it feels like looking down a long dark hole. He points at a low shelf, 'These ones have legs growing out of their heads.' He feels obscurely sorry for these flies but he supposes they don't know any different.

'Like circus freaks,' she says before she stands up straight to face him, 'do you mind if I watch you while you work?'

He does mind but he can't think why. 'I work all over the department, sometimes in here or in my office, sometimes with the new machine. You have to run to catch up with me!'

'That's fine. I'll cope.'

Later that same day he's sitting in front of the console, learning how to instruct the new machine. He hears Lucy in the office, talking to a bunch of post-docs. 'It's not ready,' she's saying, 'you'll have to wait.'

As expected, they don't believe Lucy so they come through to check with him. 'I'm still working on it,' and he gestures at the glass box, 'you'll have to wait until I'm done.' They go away again. Lucy's a good girl but she's not quite got it, not yet. She will do, given time. He's usually right about these things.

The machine's big, about two metres on each side. It's a square box supported on legs and covered with a glass canopy so you can see what's going on inside. It reminds him of an architectural model, all different shelves and levels, with metal troughs for the liquids. The row of tips suck up liquid and dispense it into the rows of wells; eight, twelve, twenty tips at a time.

'Has it got a name?' The writer is there.

'A name? No, no, not yet.' It'll acquire a name only after it's settled in, and made its characteristics known. He glances at her. From this perspective she's all angles, strong nose, hair pulled straight back off her head, long arms. Even her fingers splayed on the glass front of the machine remind him of some geometrical problem that needs to be solved. After she's wandered off to the other end of the lab he realises he still doesn't know her name either. He carries on with the instructions. Each time it's used, the machine has to work out for itself how big it is, and where all its components are. He runs through this procedure now, but something's not quite right, the metal tips crash into the bed with an audible scraping sound that makes him wince. The writer looks over, 'Is everything ok?'

'I'm learning.'

'I thought you knew everything,' and she smiles. She seems to be looking at him with a sort of tender regard similar to the way he's seen the scientists look at their flies, and he wonders if she's carrying out an experiment. And who the subject of that experiment might be.

Dinner that night is just plain nasty and sometimes he wonders if the wife does it on purpose. No wonder, he thinks as he refuses pudding yet again, that he gets up so early in the morning to escape to work.

The flies have gone wrong. It happens occasionally, no point getting worked up about it. They're more aggressive than normal so Lucy had problems doping them with the carbon dioxide, and then a test tube of them flew right into her face before buzzing off. It's the ones with the extra legs growing out of their heads and she screamed the place down. He doesn't blame her. The writer looks on as he gives Lucy a hanky.

They all stand by the window of the lab, staring at the flies banging against the glass. 'They'll die soon,' he says and this is meant to calm Lucy, but the writer replies, 'That's a shame.' She's studying the flies as if she's reading a book.

'What went wrong?' she asks him.

'Not sure.' He's thinking about how to get the lab's money back from the company who provided them.

A fly dive-bombs Lucy and she screams all over again. Perhaps she smells funny to them. The writer makes a note in her notebook.

Over dinner he suggests to the wife his plan for cleaning the conservatory roof in spring.

'About bloody time,' she sniffs. 'I've been asking you for ever.'

At least it'd get him out of the silent house in the evenings.

There haven't been any mice for a few days and he's almost forgotten about them as he walks up the silent, snow-bound corridor. She's already there, leaning against the wall the way she does, waiting for him. They don't speak. High above them, suspended from the ceiling, is a model of the double helix made out of the letters A, C, G and T. The sunlight casts shadows of the letters, making unpronounceable words that float onto the walls, the floor and her face. He's never noticed these letters until now.

On the floor at her feet is a small oval object. A nut? It's the size and shape of a large nut, but no, it seems to be a sort of squashed piece of matter. An animal turd, maybe. He squats down to inspect it.

'What is it?' he asks her.

She kneels on the floor by his side and looks closely.

'Thank goodness it's not a mouse,' he says, almost laughing. The thing has no claws, no semi-stiff tale. No obsolescent eyes.

She starts to laugh herself, 'Actually it is a mouse, in a manner of speaking. At least, it used to be a mouse.'

And then he understands. It's an owl pellet. She pulls out her phone from some obscured fold in her clothes, 'I want to take a photo of this.'

'Wait –' but she's too quick and when she shows him the photo, it's got his disembodied hand apparently floating above the lump of matter. He has a sudden and startling image of a mouse running up and down the corridor being pursued by a barn owl, white and ghost-like. He can see the dark shadow of the owl's wings caused by the strip lights above it, hear the creak of moving feathers as it beats the air. See the mouse scampering in a zig-zag this way and that, trying to dodge its death. And then after the kill – the owl standing on the floor, its talons sliding on the shiny floor as it gobbles the mouse. The tail would be the last thing to be swallowed, maybe even still flickering with life as it protrudes from the owl's beak. It feels like he's remembering this rather than just making it up. He has seen a barn owl once, silently hunting near Loch Tay, turning and turning again in the weak winter light as it searched for its prey.

'All that killing,' she says, 'just picture it.' Her words are loud in his head as if she's speaking inside him. Private words just for him. He stores the owl pellet in the drawer of his desk and goes to the lab to learn more about the machine.

When he gets home his wife isn't there. Instead there's a scrawled note propped up against the salt and pepper pots on the dining table – no doubt the traditional way of communicating these things in all those rubbishy books she reads – saying that she's gone away for a few days and his dinner's in the freezer. Even the shape of the writing manages to look accusing. It's not the first time, but when he goes to check the freezer there are more frozen boxes than ever before. Ignoring the ranks of boxes, he makes himself beans on toast and goes to eat in the green-lit conservatory, where the two of them have never eaten.

The last time she was away for a week. The time before that, a couple of nights. He wonders where she goes, but he knows he doesn't wonder enough and that's part of the problem. He sleeps well that night and wakes, feeling almost good about it all.

Later that morning he figures out what happened with the flies. When he finds the paperwork in his filing cabinet, he realises he made a typo in the gene specification. Wrong name – wrong gene – wrong flies. No matter, but Lucy's off sick now because she says the flies bit her. Seems unlikely, but he'll let her have a few more days off even if it's just nerves.

Then he remembers about the mouse traps. He hurries to inspect them. None of them contain any dead mice but, as he feared, there's an awful lot of fruit flies laying eggs and gorging themselves on the bits of Mars bars. The escaped flies have found their promised land.

He's dealing with the eggs that they've bought to replace the flies, decanting them into test tubes when the writer appears.

'You can just buy mutant flies?' She's surprised.

'Why not? You order the mutations you want, such as red eyes or curly wings, and the eggs arrive in the post.'

'Sounds a bit like Brave New World. It can't have always been like that, surely?'

'No.' And he tells her about Muller, 'There was a scientist from America in the Thirties who worked on fruit flies, and he had to leave America in a hurry because he was a Communist so he got a job in Germany, but then the Nazis came to power, so he had to leave there too and he went to Russia, but Stalin took against him, so he decided to go to Spain and fight in the civil war there. But it got too dangerous so he stayed here in Edinburgh for a bit before going back to America. And everywhere he went, no matter what happened to him, he hung onto his suitcase of fruit flies. Because he'd bred them to have particular mutations.' And he needed them, he thought. They were all he had after his first wife left him. Poor bastard. And for a moment he feels sorry for himself.

'Like a travelling fly circus.'

He doesn't like her flippant tone. 'Not exactly. It was in aid of science. He sacrificed a lot to hang onto those flies.' He's finished with the eggs so he goes to start work on the machine. She follows him and they both peer inside it as it runs through its now-routine daily calibration. It's doing a dance, he thinks, as the metal tips float move from left to right and up and down. An elegant dance that he has choreographed. There should be music.

'What are the square things with all the little holes punched in them?'

'The holes are called wells and the square things are the beds. And the shelves that they're stored on – at the back – are called hotels.' Ridiculously, he is blushing. And she's smiling at his embarrassment. Perhaps she goes to hotels with other men and gets into bed with them. A wordless image of her and him appears in his mind.

Later that night after rejecting the frozen boxes again, he lies in bed and describes the image to himself. Like the barn owl, she's swooping over him and he is naked beneath her, waiting for her to land. It is not a wholly pleasurable image, but he's able to put a word to the feeling in his gut. Desire.

A week after owl-pellet day. He's almost finished learning the ins and outs of the machine and she's at the back of the lab writing in her notebook.

'How would I go about having my genes sequenced?'

Her voice comes from behind him, her words float around

him. He thinks for a moment. 'We have a sequencer here but it's just used for the flies and for a few other experiments. We've never used it for human DNA, it would take forever. You'd be better off going to one of those companies that only do a handful of genes. They're not too expensive.' He wonders why she wants this information.

'I want to be read, I want the machine to read me.' She has seen into his mind again.

He turns to look at her and is astonished to see tears slipping down her face.

'Like a book,' he tries to joke, but still her tears keep falling until she stumbles out of the lab, presumably in search of tissues. He walks over to the corner where she's been sitting, and he picks up her notebook, thinking that it might give him some clue about her and what she's just asked him. When he glances inside at the last page she's written, at first it looks like a list scribbled in pencil with words crossed out here and there, but after a bit he starts to make it out. It's so peculiar that he makes a photocopy to take home:

<u>Go hunting</u>
take the genes of vetch
of milkweed
of toadflax
of meadowsweet
of the common or garden weed
and splice with owl
to make a ~~mutation~~ woman
who flies through the night
and grasps you in her talons
I'm the viper at your wedding
waiting to bite the bride
I'm the strands unravelled by your death
I'm alphabet matter, coded vegetation
and I will form words to be your ~~body~~ language

He was a writer, and that's why I fell for him. Plain and simple. He knew the difference between metaphor and simile, he could take a bleeding lump of raw emotion and slice thin elegant prose from it. And he predicted us, our affair was defined by his stories that had already been published. It was meant to be. I would text him to tell him what I wanted him to do and when we met in hotel bedrooms and on night trains, he would obey my words.

I killed my husband. He said I was so kind and so soft, but he used me as a pillow. He smothered himself in our marriage, and he suffocated.

Oh, there was no actual death, no funeral. It's all in my mind. But the body of the man I married has mutated. The cells I fell in love with have all died and been replaced by daughter cells. Does this explain the seven year itch, the need to be unfaithful? Why we fall in love – and fall in love again? Because we are no longer the same person?

When I was in bed with the writer he said I smelt of flowers, of roses and meadowsweet. He made me into a garland and twisted me around his body, and honey poured forth.

I fear all men and desire them, and would do anything to stop my husband crying over me. I fear them because I desire them.

I want you to look down the microscope at me and read me.

read – bead – bend – bond – bone
letter – bitter – bite – bile – cell

He manages to hide away the photocopy before she comes back to the lab. Glancing at her, he'd never guess that she's just been crying. Her face is as smooth as an egg, her eyes are clear. She looks wiped clean.

Shortly after that the owl pellet disappears, even though his desk drawer is usually locked and nobody else has the key. So all he has is the memory of finding it, and the images of her and the owl. He even keeps an eye out as he walks between the bus stop and the building each morning and evening but he never sees any owls. Perhaps they're hiding in the trees nearby. Just biding their time and waiting for the mice.

At the weekend he decides to make a start on the roof. The ladder's where he left it after the last aborted attempt, so he props it against the wall and climbs up. If he works hard, maybe he'll sleep and not lie in bed thinking those thoughts. Maybe the wife'll come back and it'll be ok this time.

The roof's worse than ever, coated with a layer of green algae that resists his fingernails and clumps of moss that have settled along all the edges. He feels disheartened. It'll take a fair amount of elbow grease to shift this lot. But he can imagine the wife's delight when she notices the full moon through the sparkling clear roof above her as she sits – as they sit together – side by side. If you're admiring a view, you don't have to speak to each other. Nature can fill in the gaps. He's seen enough couples sitting in their cars at the beach, facing the water. Some of them are old too, they've made it. They must have been silent together for a long time, it doesn't necessarily mean anything bad. It gives him hope.

He manages to clear an area about a foot square. But it still isn't great because now it looks worn and scratched. Perhaps his scrubbing has damaged it. When he peers down from the top of the ladder all he can see in the conservatory is a pile of beer cans and the remains of last night's take away.

In contrast, the machine is shiny, its metal tips so elegant as they dance through the box of air inside the gleaming glass canopy. He likes to watch the liquids shoot out of the tips and straight into the wells. The machine always gets it right now. And it doesn't need light, it has no eyes. So, one evening when everyone else has left, he turns the lab lights off, one by one, until the only way he can see his way back to the robot is from the glow of the console. He stands in the darkness touching its metal flank, and the smooth hum of its innards makes his hand tremble.

She tells him that she's sent off a sample to one of those companies. It's a crude process compared to what they can do with the sequencer in the lab, you only get a few hundred or so genes mapped out, but it's enough to say whether you're more than averagely susceptible to diabetes, whether you've got Viking heritage, and that type of thing.

A few weeks later she comes to him with the results printed on a sheet of paper which she hands over without speaking.

'This is odd,' he says, 'they've got you down as 99% likely to have red hair and blue eyes.' And you're so dark, he wants to add, but he feels shy about commenting on her looks. 'It must be wrong,' he continues, 'you should write and tell them they must have got your sample mixed up with someone else's. I'm sure it happens sometimes. It'll just be a mistake.'

'There's been no mistake,' she replies.

He never mentioned any wife or girlfriend and he wasn't gay. I invented that whole plotline about his wife walking out and him cleaning the greenhouse roof in penance. I wanted him to be single, that's why in my story his wife leaves him. But he has to care a bit, because I don't want him to be a monster. He's a caring man. I know that, because I understand him. Better than I understand myself.

I'm an iceberg. Ninety percent of me is below the surface. Diving into the cold sea, I can explore the depths – and the wrecks.

Turquoise sea, turquoise dress. The dress I'm wearing matches my eyes, swishes around my legs. Summer's just gone, and maybe it's too cold now for bare legs, but I'm sticking with the dress. I perch on a bar stool and make notes. I never stop writing, even when I'm not physically writing. I narrate my own life in my head. It's the way I am. I know that much about myself.

I spot the writer at the entrance and wave him over. Watch him walk across the bar, carefully avoiding each chair. It's crowded in here, maybe I shouldn't have chosen this place. Crowds are dangerous, there's always the worry that we'll bump into someone we know. Someone who knows we shouldn't be meeting like this and looking so happy in each other's company.

When he arrives at my stool, I tell him, 'I was in a lab today. With fruit flies and owls and dead mice—'

He laughs. He knows how I work, how I weave animals and people out of words and letters.

'Owls,' he says as he looks around for the bar staff. 'I saw an owl once. It flew right over me.'

'Was that near Loch Tay?' I ask him.

'How long have we got?' This is a few hours later. The bar is emptier, I've moved closer to him and am no longer afraid of touching his arm when I'm talking to him, just to emphasise a point. A friendly touch, nothing more. That's what I want it to look like in case anyone sees us. But a small part of me knows that the alcohol's made me uninhibited, that I'm capable of doing something stupid. I don't know exactly what, until I do it.

He looks at his watch, 'An hour or so.'

I smile. That's enough time. There's a park nearby, it's a warm night and all I'm wearing is a dress.

Afterwards I cry bitterly. Back home I sob as I sponge myself in the shower. There is a word for this behaviour, I tell myself, and that word is betrayal. I promise myself I'll never do it again. And I believe myself, because in fact it's always better before or afterwards. Never during. The actual act is fraught with panic, always uncomfortable, hardly ever that satisfying. The anticipation beforehand is better, the memories are something to relive in my mind afterwards.

'Your hair is too bright,' he whispered earlier this evening as we leant against the park wall, 'such red, red hair, my love. It shines in the moonlight.' He buried his face in it and breathed deeply. 'You smell of flowers, of roses and –'

'Did you get my texts?' I interrupted him.

'Yes.'

'Go on, then.'

So he knelt in front of me, pushing my dress up so that every part of me was exposed to the fresh night air. But I didn't feel cold. Not until now, when I'm standing in the hot shower, having to wash my body everywhere he touched it. Like cleaning up after a scientific experiment that's gone wrong. And I'm cold with shame and regret.

As usual the writer is sitting at the back of the lab, somewhere in the space behind him. They haven't discussed her genetic test and he doesn't know what she thinks about red hair or blue eyes. But now she starts to talk, so quietly that at first he doesn't realise she's talking to him.

'Once upon a time there was a woman. She met a man and fell in love and they got married. She wanted to live happily ever after. But this is a story about what happens after the fairy tale ends. Her husband expected her to iron his shirts every day, and criticised her when she ironed creases into them by accident. And then she started ironing creases into them on purpose just for an excuse to argue with him.'

He turns round, 'Is this a true story?' he asks.

'They're all true stories. Even the made-up ones.' She isn't crying but her eyes look too shiny. 'She was ironing her husband's shirts, he had a lot of shirts and it was an endless task. He wore three shirts a day and she could only iron two because she had so much else to do. So, the shirts just piled up on every surface in the house and before long they couldn't find anything else. At night time, they had to burrow into the mound of shirts on their bed, and go to sleep in them.

'Her husband was a circus master. He had a flea circus and he kept it on a mouse. It was the easiest way. That's how he moved around with his circus, he went travelling with this mouse. She was a very obliging creature and quite affectionate.

'He used to go touring with his circus, it was rather famous. And of course, the transport costs were cheap. Just a small wooden box for the mouse, and some Mars bars to feed her. He'd go off for weeks at a time. His wife was pleased because it gave her an opportunity to catch up on the ironing. She'd never actually seen the flea circus in action, she told him it made her itch just thinking about it. That was one of the many things they argued about. And when he was away she'd sprinkle flea powder all over their house, and vacuum all the soft furnishings.

'One day, disaster struck. He'd come home after a particularly long tour and he was lying down on the sofa having a nap with the mouse asleep, curled up on his chest. She used to get exhausted with all the travelling and the excitement of the circus. But the wife must have forgotten to vacuum up all the flea powder because when the man and his mouse woke up a few hours later, the fleas were all dead. Every single last one of them.

'The man was furious. He cursed his wife and she shouted at him that she hadn't married him to look after a menagerie of insects. In their anger they forgot about the mouse who had taken fright from all this noise and disappeared.

'Well, the man managed to get hold of another mouse and some more fleas and he spent months training them, but it was never the same. He'd go off touring though, and when he was away, the woman met someone else. This man was a falconer and he had a merlin, a kestrel, a sparrow hawk and a tawny owl, and they each wore little hoods on their heads. The owl had a special hood. It was made of soft black suede and had a brass bell on it.

'This man lived in a much larger house than the woman, perhaps there's more money in falconry than in flea circuses. His birds were very popular, they were good at killing rodents and he used to take them to mice- or rat-infested houses and set them loose. They were much more efficient and cheaper than poison.

'Well, the woman fell in love with this man and they had an affair while her husband was away. She would send him erotic texts and they would make love in the shed where he kept his birds. The birds couldn't see what was going on because of the little hoods on their heads, so the woman thought they were safe. She'd forgotten about the mouse that had escaped.

'One day the owl caught the mouse and ate it, and the falconer gave the resulting pellet as a sort of love token to the woman, who brought it home with her and put it in a drawer in the house. When her husband came back from his latest tour, exhausted and fed up because takings were right down, he found the pellet and recognised the remains of his old mouse. All hell broke loose and she ended up confessing to the affair.'

Silence in the lab. The Gaffer thinks for a moment, 'Is that what my owl pellet was? A love token?' He's never thought of objects as representing emotions before. Certainly not regurgitated mice.

She comes and stands by the machine again, and he stands next to her. They gaze through the glass.

'Wouldn't it be good if there was never any glass to get in the way?' He doesn't know which one of them says this, the words are in his head.

When he gets home the house is still empty but there's a note waiting for him in the kitchen, propped up against an empty beer can. It's just one sentence:

CAN YOU EVEN REMEMBER MY NAME?
He screws up the piece of paper and throws it outside into the dark garden.

She's gone. She's not at the back of the lab, her notebook has disappeared and nobody seems to know anything. Lucy's still away so he's rushed off his feet all day, but everywhere he goes in the lab is saturated with the memories of her. Outside the winter sunlight is bright and sharp so the double helix is casting word-shadows everywhere, but she's not here to catch them. Perhaps he imagined her. Perhaps she never was.

The Prof wants to have a talk about the flies. He's not happy; the company won't refund the money for the flies because it wasn't their fault, and Lucy can't come back to work here until every last one of the mutant flies has been found and destroyed. He suggests that maybe this should take priority over setting up the new machine and he reminds the Gaffer who is really in charge here. He doesn't even call him the Gaffer, he calls him by his name.

After everyone's left the lab at the end of the day, the Gaffer remains, sitting by the console and programming the machine. He's learning how to get deep into the guts of its system, so he can disable the safety features. Now the lab is dark and he can just about see the glass canopy rise up, revealing the workings. He gets up and lays his hand on one of the beds, waiting for the sharp metal tips to do what they've been instructed to do. It will be a beautiful ending.

Further information

Some of the stories in this collection were inspired by historical people and events:

The first star
In 1913 the campaign for votes for women was at its height and in May of that year the Royal Observatory Edinburgh was bombed by suffragettes, damaging the West Tower. Visitors to the Observatory can see a small fragment of the bomb. The perpetrators were never caught and it's not clear what the precise motive for this attack was. But it may have had something to do with the Observatory's short-lived practice of employing female 'computers' (the term used for people who, before mechanical computers were developed, carried out routine processing of data), and these women were always paid less than their male counterparts.

The Snow White paradox
Alan Turing first concieved of his test of artificial intelligence as essentially gender-based and this was inspired by an old parlour game, the 'imitation game'. The 'Snow White' record player as described in the story is real but here it is an anachronism because Braun, the manufacturers, didn't put it on sale until 1956. Turing always had a fascination with the story of Snow White. The first major biography of Turing ('Enigma' by Andrew Hodges) agrees with the inquest that Turing's death was definitely suicide; later biographers such as B. Jack Copeland (author of 'Turing: Pioneer of the Information Age') seem less convinced.

Heroes and cowards

Brecht's play 'Life of Galileo' was first written in 1938 and then substantially rewritten during his stay in Hollywood in collaboration with the actor Charles Laughton, who played the title role in the world premiere of the English-language version. The earlier version of the play depicts Galileo as a typically Brechtian anti-hero who is prepared to do anything to double-cross the Roman Catholic church to get his message across. But after the Manhattan project culminated in the bombing of Hiroshima and Nagasaki, Brecht wanted to update the play to show how Galileo failed to stand up to the Inquisition and thus (in his view) set a bad example for all future scientists in their dealings with authorities.

This story uses quotes from Brecht's actual evidence to HUAC. Oppenheimer's line, 'Sorry, no I can't say that I am,' is also taken from real life and was in response to a journalist asking him if he felt sorry for the use of the atom bomb. Oppenheimer did receive many awards for his work but the award ceremony in the story is entirely fictional.

Furthest South

There are several ongoing experiments to detect neutrinos based at the Antarctic. Scott's expedition of 1910-12 had many scientific purposes, and one of those was to collect eggs from emperor penguins wintering at Cape Crozier to provide possible evidence that the embryos were more 'primitive' than the fully grown penguins and therefore might provide a link between reptiles and birds. The appallingly difficult trek to obtain some eggs is vividly recounted in Apsley Cherry-Garrard's book 'The Worst Journey in the World'. This book also describes how the bodies of Scott, Wilson and Bowers were buried where they were found. There is a large wooden cross commemorating Scott and the men who died on that fatal expedition, but I've taken liberties with its location, it's actually situated at Hut Point on the edge of the continent and not near the Pole.

The equation for an apple

In 1924 J. Robert Oppenheimer travelled from Harvard to Cambridge to start his PhD in physics. But he wasn't happy there, something clearly went badly wrong and he tried to poison his PhD supervisor Patrick Blackett with an apple dipped in cyanide. This episode was subsequently hushed up by his family and the University authorities, and Oppenheimer went on to carry out his PhD work at Göttingen with Max Born. See 'American Prometheus: The Triumph and Tragedy of J. Robert Oppenheimer' by Bird and Sherwin, and 'Inside The Centre: The Life of J. Robert Oppenheimer' by Ray Monk for more information.

That sinking feeling

In the 1980s it was discovered that Einstein and his first wife Mileva Marić had had a baby before they got married. The fate of this child is not known, but it is possible she either died of scarlet fever or was adopted by friends. Einstein didn't actually live in the same apartment block as Elsa while he was still married to Mileva – that is my own thought experiment. Walter Isaacson's biography 'Einstein: His Life and Universe' is an excellent source of information.

Einstein's thought experiment in which a man in a freefalling lift experiences weightlessness was an important aspect of the development of general relativity. The words 'gravity' and 'grief' are etymologically related.

Acknowledgments

Some of these stories have already been published as different versions:

'Introduction to relativity'
in 'New Writers Awards 2012: Scottish Book Trust'

'Identity theft'
on the Human Genre Project website

'The competition for immortality'
on Lablit (http://www.lablit.com)

'Furthest South'
on CulturBooks (http://www.culturbooks.de)

'The need for better regulation of outer space'
in Fractured West, volume 5

'The voice-activated lift'
in The Scotsman

'No numbers'
was broadcast on BBC Radio 4 as part of the Shorts: Scottish Shorts series in January 2015

I'm very grateful to Andrew Crumey for acting as a mentor and providing advice and feedback on these stories as they were being written. I'd also like to thank the Scottish Book Trust for giving me a New Writers Award in 2012, and the School of Physics and Astronomy in the University of Edinburgh for letting me have office space during 2013. I'm grateful to the Hawthornden Trust for a Fellowship in January 2014 which helped me complete this collection. At Freight, Adrian Searle, Robbie Guillory and my editor Karen Campbell have helped me with huge amounts of guidance and support.

Over the past few years I've learnt lots about universes, galaxies, meteor/ites, genes, fruit flies and Antarctic exploration in conversations with Andy Lawrence, Bob Mann, Andy Taylor (who told me about the human computers at the Observatory), John Peacock, Ken Rice, Mar Carmena (who showed me her fruit flies), Lorraine Kerr (who introduced me to Armstrong the liquid-dispensing robot), Jenny Rohn, Anne Strathie, Ken MacLeod, Pedro Ferreira and Marek Kukula. Phillip Helbig gave me feedback on a number of points. Of course, any remaining mistakes are entirely my own responsibility.

As ever my lovely writing pals, particularly Mary Paulson-Ellis, Theresa Muñoz, Sophie Cooke, John Ward and Zoë Beck have all supplied feedback, good cheer, distraction and much appreciated emails.

My family Graeme Busfield, Herb Goldschmidt (who told me about Granny and the three stones) and Belle Brett are endlessly patient and supportive. Louie provided a lot of fur.